IN PLAIN VIEW LARGE PRINT

(AMISH SAFE HOUSE BOOK 2)

RUTH HARTZLER

Amish

ROMANCE BOOKS

1

HIGH POWERED U.S. Marshal, Kate Briggs, was in the back of a buggy, disguised as an Amish woman. She felt like a child, sitting in the back seat, her knees pressed tightly against the back of the driver's seat in front of her. Isaac, of course, was driving; the Amish were decidedly old school like that. Isaac's wife, Beth, made the dinner. She tended the garden, and Isaac did the manly stuff, like drive, patch the roof, and whatever else needed doing.

Kate was grateful that her boss had sent her to live undercover with the Amish for her own protection, while he tried to discover who intended her harm. At first, Kate had thought that no one would ever accept that she was Amish, yet her cover as an Amish woman with amnesia, a woman from an Amish community in another state, had worked so far. The bishop and his wife were the only ones party to the information.

Kate was staying in a *grossmammi haus* behind the large farmhouse of Isaac and Beth Kauffman, and while she at first had found the situation daunting, she was now becoming accustomed to the Amish way of life.

The farmland sliding slowly past Kate looked like the miles that had come before, and the miles that were still to come. Green fields of corn, golden wheat standing high, the tips swaying in the soft summer breeze slightly, so that it all looked like a yellow sea where the waves were lazily being pulled up toward the sun.

"Hey, who's that?" Beth called from the passenger seat, pointing her index finger.

Kate's view had given way to something other than farm fields. It was a long stretch of green grass behind a small wire fence, and in the distance was a shimmering blue-green pond. Someone was standing at the edge of the pond facing the road, waving his hands back and forth, obviously hoping to get the buggy's attention.

"Well, it's Hugh White's land, so I reckon it's him," Isaac said with a chuckle.

"It looks like you're right," Beth said, nodding her head, her bonnet bobbing slightly with the motion.

Kate did not understand how they could be so sure. From this distance, she could tell it was someone waving their hands, and that was about it. If she had to say anything about the figure, she would guess that it was a man.

Isaac pulled the buggy over to the side of the road and stopped it completely, the two wheels on the passenger side sitting off the pavement and into the dirt that bordered the wire fence. Everyone climbed out of the buggy, and Kate took the lead as they stepped down a slight dip to the fence.

"I can go see what he wants, if it's easier for you," Kate said, climbing over the small fence and turning to the older folk.

Isaac shook his head and climbed over the fence himself, and then he turned and helped Beth over as well. "Best to see what he wants," he said. "Might be trouble, might need more hands. I'm guessing one of his cows got stuck in his pond."

And indeed as they walked, they passed a few of the cows, big and black and white, their eyes large and dark and swiveling in their sockets to keep a view of the humans as they passed. Kate thought that the animals looked as if they were curious, and she hoped they would not mind trespassers through their home. One of the cows walked toward the small group of three, mooing softly, her tail swinging behind her almost like a puppy. Kate wondered if the cow would have come up and permit her to pet her, but she was too anxious to get to Hugh and see what he needed.

"I've called the police," the man said, as they got close enough to hear him. Kate thought that was a strange thing to say. "I just, err, I didn't want to leave here, but I wanted to go to the road and make sure they get flagged down."

"What are you going on about?" Isaac asked Hugh, but Kate was the first one to the man, and she looked past him to the edge of the pond and knew what he was talking about pretty quickly.

On the shore, face down, the legs sticking into the still water, and the torso and head and arms out, was a body. It was a man with brown hair, and although she could not see his face, Kate was reasonably sure he was no more than thirty five. She took a step forward, but stopped herself from moving any more than that—she had to remember not to give herself away.

"Oh my," Beth said, clapping a hand over her mouth when she saw the body. Isaac had seen it too, and he put a protective hand on his wife's arm.

"What happened?" Isaac asked. "Who is that?"

"I don't rightly know," Hugh said, shaking his head and pulling off his hat. He wiped his arm across his brow and replaced the hat. "I was just coming to check on one of the heifers, she hurt her leg yesterday. I cut through the woods there, then came around here and saw him. I didn't look too close. Then I had to run back to the barn to call the police."

Isaac turned to his wife. "Beth, why don't you walk back to the road and make sure they see us?"

Beth nodded her head at her husband's suggestion and turned away. She looked a bit green in the face, which was no surprise, as

Kate was certain that Beth had never seen a dead person before.

"Hang on there, Beth," Hugh called. "I'll go up with you."

Beth nodded, and Hugh joined her. Isaac waited until they were halfway back to the road before he spoke. "You don't seem bothered by it," he said.

Kate shrugged her shoulders, turning to look at the body once more.

Isaac kept the conversation going. "You've seen someone die?"

Kate sighed. She wasn't sure what she should to say here. She turned to Isaac and shook her head. "Die? No. But a body. My cousin, when we were younger." That, at least, was the truth.

The old man nodded. "Well, I'm sorry to hear it."

"It's all right. It was a long time ago."

Isaac nodded his head to the body on the shore of the pond. "What happened to him, ya reckon?"

Although the question seemed to be addressed more to himself than to Kate, she stepped forward a little. "I'm not sure. He doesn't look drowned, does he?"

Isaac came up beside her. "No, he doesn't."

Isaac kept walking forward, so Kate fell into step beside him. They stopped just shy of stepping onto the muddy shore. Kate was glad of that. She did not want them to leave footprints in the mud. As it was, there were no footprints around the body, which was odd. Had the man fallen? Kate looked up, and saw nothing but the blue sky of summer, and a few wispy white clouds sliding slowly along. If he had fallen, what could have been the cause?

"What's that there?" Isaac asked, pointing his finger.

Kate looked and saw what he was talking about. She bent at the knees, coming down to sit on her haunches, so she was more level with the body, but still not on the shore. On the man's right wrist was a tattoo. His arm was stretched upward, and his wrist just went past the top of his head. The tattoo was on the inside of the wrist, a black snake with the jaws wide and the fangs up high.

"A tattoo," Isaac said, squinting. "Don't see many of them around here."

Kate nodded. "No, you don't."

She stood back up and looked toward the road across the field. A white and blue police car had pulled up. It sat on the edge of the road behind Isaac's buggy, the lights on top of the car flashing red and blue. It appeared as if two cops were climbing over the fence, following Hugh back to the pond. Kate could see Beth standing near the fence, but making no effort to move.

Isaac and Kate stood waiting for the cops to make it to the pond, and when they finally did, they shook hands and introduced themselves. The cops introduced themselves as Officer Jones and Officer Saracen. Both were male and in their late twenties, both of them lean and muscular, but Saracen was short, and Jones had a brown mustache.

The cops asked everyone to step back as they inspected the body, so Kate stood with Isaac and Hugh. Something was eating at her, something in her mind pressing against her brain, a memory of something. It had to do with the tattoo. She kept thinking about it, watching as Saracen put on a white plastic glove and moved the man's arm.

And then, as memories so often do, it all came flooding back to her. She had seen that tattoo before, on two different people. Both of them were men she had worked with in WITSEC. They had been men she had hidden away. And they both had shared something else in common. They had been hitmen for the same mobster, Logan White, a big time crime boss who was nicknamed *The Viper*.

All Logan White's top men were required to get the tattoo on their wrists. No doubt it made them remember that they were loyal to Logan. Of course not everyone was loyal, and the two men Kate knew had left and tried to turn on their boss, but despite what they had given the FBI, the Feds had been unable to take Logan White down. And so *The Viper* remained, a powerful figure in New York City, and the two men who had flipped on him remained hidden away in the Midwest, unable ever to go back.

And now here was a third man with the tattoo, as dead as somebody could be. Kate watched the police officers do a quick investigation before they stepped off the muddy shore. Saracen came over to the group, while Jones went off a few steps and spoke into his radio.

"You found him then?" Saracen asked Hugh. The man nodded. Saracen had pulled a small pad from his pocket, and was writing in it. "You live here?"

"This is my land," Hugh said, pointing off toward the line of trees which grew an acre or so away from the pond. "My house is just past that, and I have a few acres over there, growing corn mostly."

"And you came over at what time?"

Hugh scratched his chin. "Well, it was an hour ago, I think. I was coming to check on one of my cows, she'd scratched her leg. I wanted to check on her, so I came through the woods by the pond and saw this man in the pond."

"And he flagged you down?" Saracen asked, turning to Isaac.

"Yes sir," Isaac said, nodding his head slowly. "He was standing out here. My wife saw him, and we stopped. He was trying to get our attention."

"You had already called us, right?" the cop asked. "Why stop them?"

"Well," Hugh said, his voice falling a little. He seemed slightly sheepish. "I just, well, I didn't want to be alone here. And uh, I wanted to go to the road and make sure you saw me, but I didn't know if that was all right, to leave him. I thought maybe an animal or something might come, or maybe he'd slide back in. I don't know, I just wanted someone else here."

Saracen nodded, working to keep his face still, although his lips twitched in an almost-smile. Kate knew that most people were uncomfortable with bodies. Police officers weren't, as a rule, although she wondered how many bodies a cop saw out here in the farm country.

"Well, my partner is calling a detective in, and a few more officers. Hugh, if you could stay, that would be great, but Isaac, you and Kate are welcome to leave."

"All right, then," Isaac said. "Are you all right here then, Hugh?"

"Yes, I reckon I am now," the man said, and he smiled. "I'm glad you stopped though. I didn't want to stand out here alone for another minute. My wife, Amy, is very upset."

Kate smiled and then turned to Isaac. "I might just stay," she said, and then suppressed a shake as the three men stared at her. "If that's okay, I mean," she added quickly. "Maybe Mr. White can give me a ride after. I know the police are here, but they'll be working, and I thought Amy might like some company."

Hugh was nodding before Kate had even stopped speaking. "Yes, that would be fine with me, if it's okay with the officers here."

Saracen shrugged as his partner Jones came over. "Sure," he said simply, and then turned to hear what Jones had to say.

"Got 'em coming, be about half an hour," he said before turning to Hugh. "Can you stay out here? They'll want to speak with you. We can send 'em to your house if you prefer."

"No, it's fine," Hugh said, but he took some steps away from the pond.

Kate felt as if she should follow him. When she stood in front of him, she smiled. "Are you all right?"

"Just shaken up, I guess," Hugh said. "You seem to be doing okay. Amy almost passed out earlier when I told her."

"I'm okay," Kate said with a slight shrug. "Iron stomach, I guess."

Kate didn't know who the man was, not exactly at least, but she knew more than she could let on. She knew he was somehow involved with The Viper, and she knew that meant he was bad news.

2

Eventually, more cars pulled up to the road, and three more officers in blue uniforms came to the pond, along with two men in suits. Kate recognized one of them. It was Detective Ryan Weaver.

"What are you doing here?" he asked Kate by way of greeting.

"We were driving by."

"Who is *we?*"

"Isaac and Beth and me. Isaac and Beth left."

"And you stayed?"

Kate nodded.

"Of course you did," Ryan said, but Kate noticed a small smile spreading on his lips. He excused himself and went to the body along with an older man who had not been introduced to Kate. They spent some time going over the scene, and then Ryan came back to Kate and Hugh.

"Do you think we could go over to your house, Mr. White?" Ryan asked. "We have some forensic guys coming, and we'll just be in the way. Just me and you, and our friend, Kate, here."

"Sure," Hugh said, nodding his head. "Follow me."

And so Kate found herself walking in step with the two men, toward the trees. Then they were going through the thin strip of woods, and when they came out on the other side, she could see Hugh's large white farmhouse. It had shutters, and a sizeable garden wrapped around one side and continued along the back of the house. Hugh's wife, Amy, was in the garden, on her knees and pulling weeds. When she realized she had company, she stood and turned. Her face was pleasant and round, her cheeks pink. She was sweating, and she pulled off a big sun hat which was over her bonnet and used it to fan her face.

"Hey there," she said in a sweet voice, and Hugh did the quick introductions.

"Well, come inside," Amy said.

They went around the side of the house and entered from the front porch. Hugh led them to the living room while Amy went to get the drinks. They waited for her to return before they got down to business.

"Does your wife know what you found out there?" Ryan asked.

"Yes, he told me," Amy said, her voice trembling. She leaned forward to set her lemonade on a coaster on the coffee table in front of her. "My word," she said, and though everyone waited for her to say more, it didn't seem as if she was going to.

Ryan broke the silence. "I just wanted to ask you all a few questions, even you, Mrs. White, if you don't mind." She said she didn't mind, so he went on. "Did either one of you see anyone on your property for the last few nights?"

"Few nights, has he been dead that long?" Hugh asked.

Ryan shook his head. "No, not that long. I would say last night is when he died, just from looking at him, but you never know about things like this. He, or someone else, could have been around here for a while."

"No," Hugh said. "No one has been here."

"Well, what about that black car?" Amy said, and her husband turned to look at her.

"Right!" he said. "We were coming home from the gathering on Sunday, and we saw a black car pulling out onto the road ahead of us. They were pulling out of one of my fields. Near the pasture actually, with the cows. There's a few dirt paths running up and down the fields, and they were coming out of one of them."

"We just figured someone had needed to turn around," Amy said. "People do it all the time."

"What kind of car was it?" Ryan asked.

"A black sedan, that's all I could tell," Hugh said.

Ryan nodded and wrote something on a pad of paper. "And this was last Sunday?"

Hugh nodded. "Right."

And so the conversation went for about half an hour. Kate listened mostly, but answered the few questions that were sent her way. By the time they were done, the glasses were empty, and everyone gathered on the front porch. Ryan shook everyone's hand. He and Kate climbed into his police cruiser and he took her back home.

Kate stood in the drive and watched the man leave. His cruiser became a small dot on the horizon and then it was gone. Ryan had barely said a word to her on the short journey.

What did this mean? She thought there had been a growing attraction between them, but then again, he thought she was an Amish woman, and Amish do not date *Englischers*.

Kate shook herself from her thoughts just as Isaac came out of the house. He stood on the porch as she went to him.

"Everything go okay?"

"Yes."

"Are Hugh and Amy all right?"

Kate nodded, and then she smiled and told Isaac that she wanted to lie down. She didn't look back as she moved along the side of the house, but she was sure Isaac was leaning over the railing to the porch and watching her go.

3

GOING for a walk was the best thing Kate could do if she wanted to clear her head, and clearing her head was her priority at this time. She could not get the murder out of her head. She had the urge to sort things out, and that was no help at all. She figured she'd be able to do better than any of the local cops could, although she had a feeling Ryan was one of those who'd do well in the city if he ever decided to move. All at once, Kate realized that her thoughts were prideful. *I'm turning Amish*, she thought with a giggle.

As Kate walked down the road, she pushed all thoughts of the murder and Ryan, from her head, focusing instead on the world around her, which was the one good thing about being dumped in the middle of nowhere.

The scents of the city were so different to the scents of the country, and Kate was beginning to think she preferred the county. She thought about how clean everything smelled without any big industry. She was beginning to understand why so many people had another home in the country. That idea was a silly one, so Kate pushed it from her mind. She did not need a home in the country. She didn't make enough to pay for one, and she still had absolutely no idea when she would be permitted to return home. What Kate needed to do was to make the most of every moment she spent in the country. She would miss it when she returned home. It was lovely to be able to walk somewhere without worrying that she might be run over by someone who wasn't looking where he was going.

It was when she was walking past the Kauffmans' pond that Kate found herself thinking about what it might be like to live in the country for the rest of her life. She knew it was a possibility that she'd be there a long time, if things didn't get sorted out, and she didn't feel like it was going to be anywhere near as much of a problem as she thought it would be at the beginning of her time in exile. Of course, the country would be far nicer if there weren't a murderer out there.

Kate really needed to call her boss, David Harper. He had given her a throwaway cell phone to use if she ever had an emergency, and right now, this sure felt like one.

Kate reached inside her Amish dress for the small pocket sewn specially to hold the phone, and finally came upon her treasure. Pulling the phone from the pocket, she called her boss and waited in anticipation.

"Hello, Kate?"

"Hi, I'm sorry to call you." The shakiness of her voice hung in the air as she tried to find the right words to use. "They found a homicide victim—the vic was found here. They found him submerged in a pond, so they can't precisely pinpoint the time of death."

"Okay, but why is telling me about that worth risking your cover?" Her boss's voice sounded frustrated, even a little annoyed.

"That's not it. The vic had a tattoo. I've seen that same one on two men, and they both turned state's evidence. The state ended up giving them immunity and putting them into WITSEC. I think someone might be trying to hunt them down."

There was silence for a moment, and then David spoke. "Tell me more."

"These guys were notorious thugs for Logan White. They were his goons, his hitmen. They did his dirty work for him, so that he could keep his hands clean."

"I see where this is going. Keep your nose clean, and I mean it. Let the local badges do their thing and keep your cover safe."

Kate knew he was right, but she was frustrated. It was hard to be a helpless girl stuck on a farm. "Understood."

"It shouldn't be much longer, I promise. It's just a bit difficult trying to track down a mole in your own organization."

"Could you at least do one thing for me then?" She knew the chances were slim, but the ever-burning determination in her heart wouldn't allow her to give up without trying. "Can you at least relay the information about the tattoo to the local police investigating the homicide?"

Silence was the response, and silence hung on the air for what seemed like an age before David finally answered. "I wish I could, Kate, but that would raise too many questions. If there were a better way I might consider it, but any direct contact with them about the case would put up red flags. Please, just let this play itself out."

Defeated, Kate exhaled slowly before responding. "Sure."

4

KATE WAS at the Kauffman farmhouse in the late afternoon, having a cup of meadow tea with Beth and Isaac, when a loud bang rattled the front door of the large home. "Just a minute!" Beth rose to her feet, excused herself politely, and walked to the door. Kate listened intently from the living room to see if she could tell who had stopped by.

"Excuse me, ma'am."

"Oh, it's you, Ryan," Beth said. "Is everything okay?"

"Yes, I actually just came by to fill you all

in with a little bit of information about the body found in your neighbor's pond. Do you and your husband have a few minutes, perhaps?" Beth must have nodded, because Kate soon after heard the door gently shut, and then Ryan followed the woman back into the room.

"Kate," Ryan said. "I wasn't expecting you to be here, but I'm glad you are. I was going to stop over at the cottage next to inform you of what we've been able to find out so far." His smile made Kate feel safe, even though she knew she wouldn't really be safe until she was back home, her real home. "Not like it's a long drive from here, but thanks for saving me the gas mileage," he said with a wide grin. Ryan sat down near Isaac and faced the two women. "Okay, here's what we know so far. We ran the victim's prints and they came back to a man named Ethan Jackson. He was from the next town over. He lived there for years, which is why it's odd that his body was found here."

Kate could not contain her impatience.

"But who is he? Does he have a record?"

Ryan looked impressed with her enthusiasm, or at least that was how she interpreted the expression that was plastered across his face at that moment. "Actually, he does. It looks like he's been a petty criminal most of his adult life. B and E's, a few charges of larceny, and here's the kicker, he was sentenced to four years, but only served a year in prison, for aggravated assault. Still not sure how he got such a light sentence given the circumstances of the case, but someone was watching out for him."

"What do you mean?" The question gnawed at Kate as she sat still, curious to know more about this man.

"I've spoken with a few other officers and detectives, and the general consensus is that he might've been involved with larger crime."

Confusion filled the room. Beth and Isaac had been silent since Ryan first sat down, but it was clear to Kate that they were trying to figure out what all this meant. "You think just because he got out of prison a little early that a gang boss pulled some strings to have him released?" Isaac asked. "I think that's a bit far-fetched, officer."

Clearly embarrassed by her husband's forthright words, Beth stood up immediately. "Would anyone like some tea or lemonade?"

"Yes ma'am, if you wouldn't mind. I could use a nice glass of something fresh before I get back to this investigation." Ryan smiled sweetly as Beth left for the kitchen, and then turned toward her husband. "Isaac, I don't know all the facts yet, but we just aren't sure. Right now, a lot of what we think is just conjecture, but some of it makes sense."

"Are you leaving something out?" Kate said demurely, knowing full well that he had to be.

Ryan shifted uncomfortably in his seat before answering. "All right. Look, don't say this to anyone else, please. The main thing we have to go by, right now, is a tattoo found on the victim. Using a photograph of the vic, I cross referenced that and his tattoo with the

Gang Unit's database of criminal aliases, and that's how we found out what they called him on the streets. I don't want that information to be made public yet, so I really can't say it, but with everything else, it just seems like this guy got in too deep with the wrong crowd and was taken out. Now we just have to figure out why he was targeted, and who did it."

"Who ordered the hit," Kate said without thinking.

Ryan nodded at her in agreement. "We don't know if that's the case yet, but it might be."

At that point, Beth returned to the living room with a tray of cups and some fresh lemonade. She poured everyone a glass before sitting back down beside her husband. "I haven't heard everything you were talking about," she said, "but I still can't believe this is happening so close to home."

Ryan shook his head. "Petty criminals are one thing, but we're concerned he might've been involved in gang activity."

"Gang activity," Kate said, "or organized crime?"

Ryan seemed to be caught off guard by her statement. "Organized crime? Whatever made you say that?"

Kate thought quickly. "Back home, my best friend went on *rumspringa* and watched a lot of crime shows on TV. She always told me about them, even though I didn't want to hear."

"Oh, that's wonderful!" Beth exclaimed, leaning over to grasp Kate's hand. "You're getting your memory back."

Ryan remained silent, so Kate smiled at Beth and continued. "He has a tattoo that is probably delegated to members of some sort of group, and you haven't gone into detail about the cause of death, so I'm guessing it was an execution."

Ryan chuckled. "You sure are a smart girl. Especially for someone who has grown up around chickens and cows, and corn and cabbage."

"My friend was always going on about criminal cases." Kate smiled sweetly, and shot a glance at the three present. None of them seemed at all suspicious.

Ryan paused for a moment and then stood up. "Thank you all for your time and hospitality. I will be sure to let you know of any future developments."

Isaac stood up. "Do you think the crime has come out as far as our community?"

Ryan shook his head. "No, if anything, the organized crime syndicate is opening up in the vic's town of residence, not here. But, since the corpse was found so close, I just want you to be on alert and let me know directly if anything happens or if you see any suspicious people around your property."

"Of course," Isaac and Beth replied in unison.

As Ryan walked toward the exit, Kate followed closely behind. As he opened the door and stepped out, she caught the doorknob with her left hand. "So, are you going to find out what's going on? It sounds pretty dangerous."

"I was about to say, *Danger is my middle name*, but that's probably a bit too cliché, eh?" Ryan winked at Kate.

She couldn't help but laugh. "It does sound bit corny. Anyway, be careful, won't you."

At that moment, something passed between them. Kate was unprepared for the uncomfortable feeling that followed, so she spoke to break the moment. "Although I'm not from this community, I've grown close to Beth and Isaac, and their daughter Rose," she said. "I don't want anything bad to happen to them."

Ryan nodded. "I promise you, Kate, whatever I find out, you'll be the first civilian to know about it."

She smiled sweetly. "Thank you, Ryan. I appreciate it."

Ryan slowly disappeared into the day as he got into his cruiser and drove off, leaving only dust from the dirt road behind him.

Kate stood in the doorway after he was out of sight, and contemplated her next move. Something big was happening; she could sense it. The next step would be to find out more about the victim. How was he involved in organized crime, and why was he killed? Those two questions would be at the forefront of the investigation, her investigation, at least. *That tattoo is more important than these cops will ever know*, Kate thought. She had her hunches, but until something else came to light, Kate wanted to remain optimistic.

Although she was hiding from her past life, it felt like it was still hunting for her. And now, it was closing in. What if someone she had dealt with as a Federal Agent happened to see her? The fear trickled down her spine, but her courage and determination halted it in its tracks. "I'm not going to let you ruin this town," she said under her breath as she shut the door.

5

KATE TRIED NOT to grimace as she studied
the hopeless white knot balanced between her
two oversized needles. This was ridiculous.
She had graduated in the top five of her class.
She was qualified to handle high level
equipment. She was part of over a dozen
highly classified cases with complex
procedures. Surely she would not be bested by
two sticks and an oversized string.

Nevertheless, Kate had begun to enjoy the
Amish knitting circle days. She glanced
around at the circle of baby dresses, intricate

blankets, and perfectly stitched socks the other ladies were crafting as they chattered away about the community. Naomi was going to make her much-loved jelly, with Gloria helping her. Lillian was fussing about how her husband was tilling the field on his own again, not wanting to disturb their nephew to share the workload.

The smell of a berry cobbler was seeping in from the kitchen. Kate swallowed as her mouth watered. Sweet things all had to be made from scratch in this community, the old fashioned way. While a berry cobbler wasn't a Spiced Latte with cream, it was the next best thing in this place.

She pulled out her needles from the mass of wool and tried to untangle the wool as best she could. *This place wasn't so bad once you got used to the whole thing*, Kate thought. She still wanted many conveniences from her old life, of course. Microwaves, for example. A single-serve coffee pot. Bottled soda. But those cravings were getting less painful as time went by.

Some things never changed though. Like crime. And undercover or not, the agent in her was going crazy over the fact she could not work on the case at hand openly. She wondered how much longer it would be before they found the mole. The sooner she could get back out there to her old life, the better.

Kate thought back to the tattoo that had been on the victim. She wondered if his presence was in some way connected to the mole. Of all the crime rings that could have shown up in this tiny quiet area, it had to be one of the most classified and elusive ones on which she had ever worked.

And to make things all the more vexing, she was stuck playing an Amish woman with amnesia. She should not have any personal interest or knowledge of a top secret crime ring. These guys were no rookies. They practically danced circles around the law, and had their hands in major criminal activities in at least three major cities, as well as some number of small towns if her hunch was correct.

Of course actually checking out her hunches without blowing her cover was just shy of impossible.

"You'll figure it out, Kate."

Kate jumped in surprise at Lillian's voice, causing the older woman to jump too, and to laugh nervously at Kate's reaction. "Goodness, Kate. You're going to get wrinkled up if you keep fretting over that project. The world won't end if you can't remember how to knit."

Kate forced a smile as she studied the mess in her lap. "There's just a lot on my mind. That's all."

"Like what?" Esther asked as she gasped and leaned forward. "Did you start to remember something about before your accident?"

"Oh no. Nothing like that. I'm afraid I'm not any closer than when I got here," Kate said quickly, feeling her face color. It wasn't that she was shy with crowds. Quite the contrary. She knew how to work a crowd back in her hometown. But here, people paid so much attention to *you*, rather than your station or job title. The Amish were so aware of individual strengths, weaknesses, body language, and quirks. Kate figured that someone like ninety year old Naomi would put lie detectors and profile experts to shame with how observant she was.

Kate glanced in the older woman's direction. As expected, Naomi was frowning as she studied Kate from across the room. Kate suspected that Naomi knew from the start she was hiding something from them. But the woman never brought it up, and Kate was at a loss on how to confirm her suspicion.

"Do you think you will ever..." Esther began, just as a breathless Beckie rushed through the door grasping a whirlwind of yarn and an over-sized blanket. The woman had been in such a rush that her bonnet was flapping haphazardly against her back, and her hair was falling out in wisps from the once-neat bun at the base of her neck.

"I'm sorry I'm late," Beckie gasped. She flopped into her chair as all eyes focused on her. She unceremoniously dumped her basket of supplies onto the floor. "You won't believe what I just heard."

Lillian gasped. "Was der schinner is letz?" *What on earth is wrong?*

Beckie waved a hand frantically to fan herself, while Lillian rushed to get her a glass of water. Kate breathed a small sigh of relief as the attention was now focused on Beckie for the time being. Kate did not know how much longer she would be able to play on the amnesia thing, given people were getting more emboldened about trying to help jog her memory by prying for details about her supposed community. They were careful not to be indelicate about the small details they thought they knew, but it was surely a matter of time before they started to suspect something was wrong.

"There's a crime ring in the next town over," Beckie declared.

Kate's jaw dropped, but luckily, her expression was hidden amongst the other shocked gasps and startled whispers between the ladies.

"Really, Beckie," Maria scolded the woman. "First you show up late, then you get everyone riled up with idle gossip?"

"It's not gossip," Beckie insisted, before gulping down half her glass. "My cousin, Jeremiah, saw them with his own eyes. He's on *rumspringa*, you know."

Beckie, clearly ignoring Maria's stern disapproving looks, scooted to the edge of her seat. "They are a right nasty group too. Jeremiah says they have connections in the town's political structure. Jeremiah is staying with some people who run their own café. These thugs started shaking the family down for protection money. When the man said the mayor would run them out, the leader just laughed and said they own the mayor. Jeremiah told me that he thinks that they have people in the police force, and judges already, too. No one even acknowledges complaints."

"Es waarken maulvoll gat!" *There's nothing good about that!* Lillian covered her mouth with delicately curled fingers. "What has this world come to, these days?"

"He really should come on back home," Esther said. "I know this is his time, but it's dangerous out there."

"That's not even the scariest part of the story." Beckie was all but bouncing in her seat. "That photo of man the police showed us? The man found in the pond? That man was the one shaking down that family for money."

"How could you possibly know that?" Maria asked, looking torn between shutting down the woman's story and listening.

"Because Jeremiah saw the dead man's picture in the newspapers. And he's the exact same man who shook the cafe down for money. Twice that he knew of."

Kate was surprised. She was sure that agents would have given themselves headaches trying to figure out how to find out that information, yet Beckie had effortlessly gotten all that information from her cousin. *That's it —forget the Feds*, Kate thought. *When I get back to my real life, I'm going to hire an Amish knitting circle.*

Lillian looked around the room and twisted the scarf she was working on in her hands. "My brother nearly got run into on his way to market the other day. That was the day before they found the body. He said two cars came through the main trail going awfully fast. If he hadn't scooted this horse to the side in time, they would have smashed clear through his buggy. He said it looked like one was chasing the other."

This brought on a fresh wave of whispers and gasps. The town road was not far from the community at all. And the man had been found in a pond right there.

"Do you think that was the man who died, and the ones who killed him?" Esther asked as the women started to whisper among themselves.

"Goodness gracious, Lillian. Your brother had *Der Herr* watching out for him then," Abigail said, her face white.

"No doubt about that," Esther chimed in. "Why didn't you say anything?"

"I thought it was just some mindless teenagers from town or something."

Naomi banged her cane against the wooden floor, sending the women into immediate silence. Despite her age, the woman commanded immediate respect. "All right, ladies. There's no use speculating about things we have no control over."

"That's right," Maria said, recovering her composure and stern expression. "We're not here to be a bunch of gossiping hens. One minute it's news about Jeremiah having an encounter, next you are all letting your imaginations run wild."

Maria rose to her feet and neatly placed down her knitting as she sniffed and headed toward the kitchen. "It should be about time for the cobbler to come out of the oven. I'll prepare the plates. Beckie, would you help me with the drinks?"

Beckie agreed as she struggled to her feet, but the fact that she was disappointed that Maria was pulling her away from continuing the hushed gossip, was as plain as day.

Kate frowned and tried to look busy with her knitting as she thought about the details. The crime ring had some sort of connection to the mayor. The dead man had been shaking down town businesses for protection fees. And he was found dead in a pond the day after they nearly ran over Lillian's brother. That about summed it up. If she had her badge, she'd be having a hay day with this rush of information. But how to do it as Kate, the amnesic Amish girl?

"Is your brother okay?" Kate asked Lillian, trying to think of any details he might have told her about the car chase. If it had been right before the murder, then there could potentially be some vital clues in their stories.

Lillian turned her attention to Kate. "*Jah*, Benjamin is fine, *denki*. He was a mite shaken up over the whole thing, but that is it."

Kate was about to work out an innocent enough request for details when she saw the gears turning in Lillian's head.

"You know, Kate," Lillian started speculatively. "My *bruder*, Benjamin, well, I think he might have an eye on you. You and he ought to take a little buggy ride together. How would you feel if he happened to ask?"

Esther reached over to smack Lillian on the knee. "Lillian! You can't just go pushing your brother on poor Kate. She might have herself a fiancé back home she still needs to remember."

"Well then, she should break it off with him for not coming by all this time," Lillian shot back in an indignant tone. "She can't remember what doesn't come visiting. And we all know there's plenty of eligible *menner* that would come courting if Kate gave them half a hint she was looking."

"But I'm not looking," Kate said. She was startled and her mind was whirling. How in the world did they go from a crime ring to her love life? Or lack thereof?

Lillian smiled mischievously. "Well, you can just look. Having a little attention now and then never hurts anyone."

Esther shook her head. "Oh let her be, Lillian. Kate, don't fret over it. Lillian is just teasing you a bit. Don't pay it any mind."

Kate smiled, but already her thoughts were drifting away. The sooner she could solve the case, the safer these ladies would be. If organized crime got their claws too far into the town, an occasional burglar would be the least of this Amish community's problems.

6

As the sun shone through the window, illuminating her bedroom, Kate rolled over, partially waking up from the intrusion of light that crept into her tightly closed eyes. She rubbed her eyes furiously and forced herself to wake from her deep slumber. After struggling to avoid getting out of bed for several minutes, she finally rolled out of bed and walked into the kitchen. She put on the coffee and then started to make scrapple.

When Kate had first arrived in the community, she had done her best to avoid the mixture of meat and cornmeal, but now she looked forward to the breakfast meal. She had even become used to not having electricity, and was becoming accustomed to the slower pace of life.

Yet Kate was still was not comfortable driving the buggy, despite the fact that she had done so many a time. Today, she had to drive Rose to town so Rose could work in a quilt store for several hours, and the thought of driving the buggy was making Kate's stomach churn. She thought of asking Rose to drive, but it was expected that the she, being the older woman, would be the one to drive.

Later, while Kate was walking around town, trying to keep herself entertained while waiting for Rose, she stopped in a small café and ordered coffee, this time a spiced chai latté. *I feel almost normal again*, Kate thought, drinking a latté and watching the television affixed to the wall.

The local news report was on, talking about such things as the weather, and some cats stuck in a tree, and a bank robbery in another county. None of that interested her, but then something she heard definitely caught her attention. The narration of a breaking news report echoed through the café.

"Good morning, I'm Maria Mandalay, reporting for Channel 7 news. Today we are bringing you an update on an ongoing investigation. Last week we reported that a man was found lifeless in a resident's pond. Police have now released the victim's name. He is a thirty-four year old man by the name of Ethan Jackson. Police are also reporting today that new evidence in the case is being examined. A 2007 Lincoln Continental was found crashed into a tree near a back road just south of the park and approximately one hundred yards from where the victim's body was recovered. Stay tuned to Channel 7 for more updates on this breaking story."

Kate listened intently to the shocking report. She knew there was a good chance that the car had probably been towed back to the station to be inspected and tested for evidence by now, but perhaps there could still be some sort of clue that could point her in the right direction. She didn't have an exact location, but she had a good idea of the general vicinity of the site of the car wreck.

Kate walked out to the buggy and untied the horse, patting his glossy neck before climbing aboard the buggy. After trotting for some time, the buggy arrived at the park that had been mentioned in the news report.

Kate drove around, looking for any signs of a tree that could have been hit recently. Other than some poorly trimmed bushes and an abandoned sneaker that hung from an electrical wire, nothing seemed out of place in the slightest. She circled the area several times and decided to head toward the neighbor's land where the body was found. Just a few minutes later, she came upon a clearing right by the side of the road. Some ribbons of caution tape blew in the wind, still wrapped around a barely standing tree. Its bark was severely scuffed, and there were some large, broken branches dotting the ground beneath it. This had to be where the car was found.

Kate carefully tied the horse to a tree well away from the road, and looked around the scene. She noticed several shards of glass decorating the ground and some deep tire impressions in the soft earth. Crouching down on one knee, she carefully examined the marks, but she knew they would be of no help to her. The police already knew the make and model of the vehicle, so the tires would surely match it, she thought. "Hmm," she said softly.

Kate was startled by the sudden low buzzing of what appeared to be some type of music. She looked around, but could see nothing that could be emitting such a sound. There were no cars on the desolate, forgotten back road. The ringing continued, so Kate walked toward the source of the noise.

As she approached the melody, Kate realized it was coming from a large set of bushes located several yards away from the damaged tree. Making her way over, she peered between a few short branches, hoping to catch a glimpse of the source of this unexpected music. To her surprise, what appeared to be a small electronic screen lit up and rumbled as the device danced to the rhythm of the ring tone. It was an abandoned cell phone that must have been discarded there recently. Kate reached in through the sharp, needle-like leaves of the evergreen shrub, seized the phone, and pulled it from its hiding place.

Kate looked around to make sure nobody had been watching her, and then decided to head back to the buggy and examine the newly discovered cell phone in privacy. Once she was back inside the buggy, Kate tried to look through the phone. However, there was an obvious problem—it was locked, and to get in, she needed to swipe the touch screen interface in a specific order and pattern. After trying for some time to connect the dots in the correct sequence, Kate became more and more frustrated as attempt after attempt failed.

Finally, just as she was about to give up, she noticed it was possible for the sequence to outline a letter. First she used her finger to trace a Z—nothing happened. Then, she tried a Y—definitely not. "This is so frustrating," she said aloud. Right before she placed the phone down, Kate had the urge to try just one more time. After she swiped a V from left to right, the phone unlocked, giving her free access to the device and all of its contents.

The first place she looked for clues was the phone's photo album. As she scrolled through several images, a clear portrait of a man who was most likely the victim appeared. Because it was taken in the manner of a selfie, she assumed that the phone must have belonged to the victim. Reinforcing her claim, the man's social media sites were all linked, proving the identity of the cell's owner.

Maybe she could find a contact who would

be willing to give her some information about the guy and with whom he was involved. Yet the list of names and phone numbers was long. How would she know just who to contact? It was like looking for a needle in a haystack, and the haystack just kept growing.

Kate decided to look through a few more screens on the phone, when an app caught her attention. It was named, *Record-a-Call*. How odd. Opening it up, a splash screen welcomed her back, and then revealed a list of saved files which looked like recordings. Each file was labeled with a contact, followed by what appeared to be a date and time.

The newest recording was entitled *Lucas_03_15_01:32*. With curiosity building, Kate tapped the track and listened closely to what came next. The snapping of twigs could be heard, as the voice yelled into the phone. "Yo man, I need your help!" The voice subsided and all that could be heard was static before the sound of more rustling.

"Hello? Hello? I can't hear a word you're saying. What's up?" another voice replied.

In broken phrases, the caller continued. "Service out here is bad...man...but... I'm being chased. I think it's W..te's men. Can you hea... Hello?"

The service seemed to keep dropping here and there, making the conversation difficult to comprehend. Then, the other voice spoke again. "I knew tho... uys... ere gonna come aft... you."

It was enough to give Kate a headache, but she kept listening closely. After nearly thirty seconds of silence, a new voice crackled over the speaker.

"Logan White sent us looking for you. Your double dipping stops here." A loud bang ended the recording. In a state of horror and shock, Kate sat in silence for several minutes. Not sure what to do, she listened to the phone call once more. Kate realized this was indeed a professional hit. And Logan White, *The Viper*, the notorious crime boss, of all people!

Unsure of what step to take next, Kate clicked the horse into a trot and headed back to town.

Kate still had time before Rose would return, but after she parked the buggy and tied up the horse, she climbed back into the buggy to think over what to do. The thought of taking the phone to the police station was on her mind, but she could not afford anyone questioning her as to how she had come across it. Further, her identity could be called into question if anyone were to dig into her background.

Holding onto the phone was out of the question, even if it was her next idea. Not only would it look bad if it were somehow to be found in her possession, but it would also be withholding crucial information from an ongoing investigation. That simply was not a valid option. Then, her next idea struck a chord. Why not mail it in anonymously?

Kate got out of the buggy and walked through town until she came to a little stationery store, where she found the idea piece of stationery. She pulled out a manila envelope that was insulated with bubble wrap. She knew that would be perfect, and it was no larger than a folded sheet of paper.

Kate took the envelope back to the buggy, where she wiped her prints from the phone. Kate placed the phone inside the envelope, and sealed it with the self-seal sticker. The last thing she needed was to have her DNA floating around on an envelope that contained evidence in a murder case.

Kate knew that sending something in the mail without a return address could be tricky, so she wrote down the address of the fire station that was located close to the police precinct. If the envelope got lost or had to be returned to its sender, she was sure the fire department would be the best bet, as they would most likely take it to the police station after receiving it.

As Kate set off to post the letter, the facts of the case rushed through her thoughts. Who exactly was Ethan Jackson, and how was he linked to the two men she had dealt with when she was Federal Agent? And who was the Lucas guy that the victim had tried to call for help? Nothing made any sense. All she knew was that something bad was invading the innocent community, and she could not let that happen.

Kate stopped at the first mailbox she saw, and gently dropped in the phone, while letting out a sigh of relief. "Let's hope you find your way," she said.

7

KATE FOUND herself back in town at the end of the week. She had asked Beth if she could borrow the buggy for the day, and Beth had agreed, stating that Kate needed to get out and about. The Amish community had a nice quiet charm that Kate was learning to appreciate. Yet the town itself was much closer to her comfort zone. The sights and sounds had an almost nostalgic feel to them. She missed the hustle and bustle of keeping the streets relatively safe. She missed the late nights and the early mornings dealing with witnesses.

It was nice to get out and stretch her legs now and then, and with a crime to solve, she felt a lot closer to home. It would have been nice to have a tablet or something with which to search through databases in a WiFi hotspot. Yet it wouldn't be the first time she had to make do with what she had.

Where to start was the question. Kate needed to check through newspaper archives to find out how much the public in general knew. She needed to scan through public records of the victim.

Kate's stomach growled as the smell of fast food and charred meats caught her attention. She thought that a club sandwich with fries was sounding pretty good right now. A soda, perhaps, a big Cherry Pepsi. It didn't even have to be a diet one.

Kate was going to need to do a little therapy shopping before she went back. Some sweetener and coffee flavoring in particular. The world always looked better with coffee. In fact, there was a rather nice looking café right on the corner. Kate decided to get a good lunch and then start into her work. It would be refreshing to pretend she was back to her normal life for a little while. But first, she needed a club sandwich and Pepsi.

The café was very quaint, although after the weeks in the community, the noises of town were almost overwhelming. Kate tried to remember if ring tones and cooking instruments had always been so loud, and if people had always been in such a hurry.

She could smell a whole host of different foods in the air. The booths were all filled with patrons eating and chatting away amongst one another. Near the doorway, she saw people with a laptop, a tablet, several notebooks, and various folders scattered across their table. It was not that long ago that she would have been one of those people. It had been part of her normal routine. And ironically, she was always telling herself she needed to slow down.

Then when I slow down, I am constantly wanting to be back out there full throttle, Kate thought, smiling at herself.

As Kate moved to the counter to place an order, she noticed a familiar face. Tall, dark, handsome. Five o clock shadow. What was Ryan doing here? Granted this town was where he lived, worked and patrolled, but out of all the places to eat in town, why here?

It wasn't that she didn't like him, far from it. The problem was that he was way too sharp for his own good. She could not afford for him to take too much of an interest in her comings and goings. She could not afford for Ryan to become skeptical of the amnesiac Amish girl routine. The last thing she needed was for him to get curious enough to ask the wrong question, get a wrong hunch, and start looking into her non-existent community. She doubted her boss would appreciate her getting her cover blown by being too careless with a small-town detective.

That was the last thing Kate needed while trying to solve a case on the sly. *Why was it that you always run into the one person you do not want to see when you go into town?* she silently asked herself. Go without makeup and sweat pants, there are two of your colleagues in the same checkout line. Trying to go undercover? There's the one guy who could complicate things right there!

Maybe a tactical retreat was in order. There were other cafés out there. Kate could even try to hunt down the one where Beckie's cousin, Jeremiah, was staying. Food and a chat in one step. She could find out details about the whole protection business over lunch and kill two birds with one stone. She also needed to be on her A-game on her investigation this afternoon. It wasn't like she was trying to avoid Ryan. Okay, perhaps she was trying to avoid him a little.

Squaring her shoulders, Kate took a deep

breath. She was going to get her Pepsi and something good to eat. And maybe she should talk to Ryan. Maybe she would find out something about the case. Well, that was unlikely, but still worth a shot.

"Good afternoon!" she said, causing Ryan to look up, surprised, from his burger. She noticed right away that he looked on the haggard side. She knew the look very well— one too many frustrating, late nights. He looked a little puzzled seeing her in front of him.

"Ah, Kate. How are you?" Ryan asked as he smiled widely at her. "Won't you join me? Keeping out of trouble?"

"I do try." Kate gave a well practiced smile that hopefully laid on the charm of a friendly Amish woman, as she sat opposite him. She was doing better with her position, but she still had a way to go to make her role natural. "How is the case going? Have you managed to find out what happened with that poor man?"

"Sorry, Kate, I can't give you any details

other than the ones I've already given you," he said.

Kate looked at the dark circles under his eyes. He looked like he had only gotten an hour or two's sleep at best. "That bad, huh?" She grimaced in sympathy. She knew what it was like to live on two hours' sleep on a frustrating case, with bosses constantly nagging for progress. False leads. Dead ends. She had her fair share with the crime ring he was trailing. In fact there still begged the question if he even knew it was a crime ring yet.

"Pretty bad, yes." Ryan gave a thin smile as he nodded in agreement.

Kate was upset. Apparently the phone had been less than helpful. Either that, or no one in the station made the right connections.

"That's a shame." She tried her best to hide her disappointment. This problem needed to be fixed before the crime ring really got its hooks into the area. She could imagine bodies appearing in the back fields of the

Amish farmers. The ring certainly didn't care much about leaving their mess in a pond by the road. So then, how long would it be before they started showing up in barns and doorsteps?

But how to get the locals to pick up and get moving on this case? She wanted to call her boss, but he had made it clear that she could not use the emergency phone to try to bring in federal help. There was also the distinct risk she would run into someone she knew during the investigation, ruining her cover. No, she couldn't pull in the professionals, even if they were best suited for the problem.

"May I help you?" Kate turned at the voice to see a young lady waiting patiently for her order. She checked the menu, and was happy to find that they did indeed serve Pepsi. No cherry Pepsi, but she was willing to settle.

By the time she finished making her order, Ryan looked a little surprised. His brows were raised slightly as he regarded her.

"It's not against the rules to eat out," she said, giving him an amused smile. She had the excuse of never dealing with the Amish before she came here. She felt a little better about her ignorance knowing the town locals were not much better. "Some of the Old Order Amish beg to differ sometimes. But we're really not all that different from anyone else."

"Sorry, you're right," he said agreeably, although as usual, he seemed to be trying to puzzle her out. "So what brought you to town?"

Oh dear, she had forgotten to work out that cover story. Time to think fast! "I'm meeting a friend here. We're going shopping for yarn and some new knitting needles. I got here early, so I thought I'd come in and get some lunch."

"I see," Ryan said, although he looked as if he didn't quite believe her. She could not tell if he was suspicious of her, or if he always looked that way. It would really help if she could get into his head and figure out what thoughts were running around in there.

"I do enjoy the knitting circle," she continued, putting on an innocent voice. "The ladies are so lovely to talk to. Oh, one even said her cousin had a close encounter with a crime ring the other day."

"Is that so?" Ryan did not appear interested.

Nevertheless, Kate proceeded to tell him some of the details she had gathered in the knitting circle. She even added some irrelevant details about knitting and the ladies to give her ramble more authenticity.

Ryan scrambled to grab a napkin and hunt down a working pen to write down details. She enjoyed the impatient, excited gleam in his eyes as he tried to guide her back onto the topic each time she tried to ramble about knitting or one of the ladies. It was fun being on this end of an official chat.

Kate found herself enjoying her meal as Ryan got every detail he could, although of course she was careful to give the details inefficiently. She was a clueless civilian after all. As much as it pained her to have to leave most of her actual knowledge out of the conversation, she had an image to keep. And after a lengthy fretting over what would be the best cake for her turn to serve the knitting circle, she had a feeling he was a far less suspicious of her civilian status.

They talked a little more, but as expected, Ryan excused himself to go elsewhere. Kate sighed contently and finished her meal.

It was early afternoon when Kate made her way back home.

After Kate rubbed down the horse and fed him, she saw Beth taking in her laundry. She waved as she approached, quickly moving to help take the clothes off the lines. While Kate hated doing laundry without a modern washing machine, she did love the fresh scent of the air dried sheets. She especially loved the scent of the towels which Beth always dried on the lavender bushes.

"How was town, Kate? You were gone quite a while." Beth folded a sheet and put it in the bottom of her basket.

"It went well. I spent most of it walking around."

Beth nodded. "That's wonderful, dear. Getting out and seeing people should be wonderful for your condition."

Kate noticed that Beth seemed excited. "Did anything happen while I was gone?" she asked.

"I found a letter from Rose," Beth said in a conspiratorial whisper. "To Samuel, that is. And knowing her, she'll never send it to him."

"I see."

"Would you help me out, Kate?"

Kate blinked, puzzled over the sudden request. "With what?"

Despite the fact that they were the only two people there in at least half a mile, Beth smiled and leaned in close. "I've invited Samuel over for dinner. I need you to help me get Rose and Samuel together."

Kate gave an uncomfortable smile. "Of course I will. I don't think I'm any good at matchmaking, though." The look of profound disappointment on Beth's face made Kate feel guilty. "You know what? Now that I think about it, I'm sure I can be of some help," Kate amended quickly.

Her comment seemed to perk Beth up. Beth chatted on about the details excitedly as she and Kate finished folding the laundry.

8

KATE APPROACHED THE TALL, decrepit apartment building where the homicide victim, Ethan Jackson, was reported to live. The address was 206. Since that probably meant his apartment was on the second floor, Kate walked around the exterior until she saw a fire escape leading up one level. Leaping into the air like a grasshopper in the fields, her hands gripped the cold, wrought iron rung and she hoisted herself up onto the ladder. She slowly climbed to the landing and approached the window.

Kate hoped no one had seen an Amish woman shimmying up the ladder.

Since the victim wouldn't be coming home, Kate expected the apartment to be vacant. She attempted to open the window; it slid upward with ease. Weird. In this type of neighborhood, she was sure the windows should always be locked. She slipped inside, and when she turned around, she noticed a half-full gallon of milk sitting beside a spilled puddle of the liquid on the kitchen counter. Weird again. It was almost like someone left in a hurry.

Deciding she had no choice but to ignore the peculiarity of the situation, Kate chose to focus on the goal at hand. She entered the living room and saw a laptop sitting atop a wooden computer desk. She plopped into the comfortable chair and relived city life for a brief moment. She opened the laptop and tried to log on. *Access denied.*

Frustration seeped in as she tried to refocus. She pressed a few buttons in unison and a prompt bleeped onto the bios screen. She tapped away at the keys until another window opened, asking her to confirm that she wanted to continue. She pressed *Yes*. Suddenly, the screen flashed before a green text littered the screen: *Access granted*. She was in.

Sifting through the man's files, Kate came across an assortment of photographs, music files, pirated movies, and everything else one would expect to find on the computer of a middle-aged hitman. She opened up his web browser and clicked the mailbox icon from his homepage. She looked more closely and noticed the email user's account name: *EvilSnake143*. Odd, considering that Logan White was known as *The Viper*. Kate began searching through his emails. One after another, she read through spam mail, news from his favorite websites, and some conversations with a girlfriend.

After a few more sweeps of the computer, Kate realized it held nothing of importance. It made sense to her that no information of his extortions existed on his hard drive, as it was highly unlikely that hitmen conducted their business online. Through her dealings with those types of men in the past, she knew they were a highly suspicious group. They left nothing to chance.

When Kate turned her attention to the bedroom, she noticed several things seemed out of place. The drawers of several dressers were left half opened, and the closet was also left open, with clothes strewn all across the floor. It was starting to make her think that maybe she wasn't the only one who had snooped around the victim's apartment.

Kate knew the police had been there, of course, but they would not have been so careless with the scene. Milk left sitting on the counter, tussled drawers and clothing, and most likely coming in through the window: what type of cop would do those things? None that she had ever worked with.

Continuing her inspection, Kate walked

into the kitchen for the first time. She had noticed the milk earlier, but failed to examine the area closely at the time. The milk was still cold when she placed her finger against the container. To her trained eyes, it looked like someone had made themselves at home, ransacking the apartment, looking for information, and even pouring a nice, refreshing glass of whole milk before they were somehow interrupted.

Kate approached the closet doorway, and peeked in to see a room littered with the ultimate biker's bedroom. Leather jackets were draped over a large sofa, with posters of rock and roll favorites scrawled out along the walls. As she looked around, she heard the sound of metals scraping against each other in the direction of the front door.

Click... the door swung open and she pulled her head back inside the bedroom.

Kate hid behind the door, hoping the intruder wouldn't come looking where she was. Suddenly, Kate heard the chatter of a police radio as it cackled to life. "This is dispatch, please go 55."

An all too familiar voice answered. "10-4, on location now." The man continued walking through the apartment, when his footsteps grew closer to Kate's location. One by one, each step grew louder, so she crept backward toward a wooden door. It was an odd-looking door. It was thin, and its face resembled window blinds, with countless slits in the wood, allowing someone to look out from inside the room, but looking in, you could see nothing but the solid, oak door. Kate grasped the doorknob in her hand and without looking, withdrew into the narrow room. Pitch darkness surrounded her.

Kate realized the room had no windows, so the light from the sun could not reach the inside. The smell of the room tickled at her nose. It was odd and peculiar, something she had never smelled before. Her curiosity ceased when she heard the steps outside the blinded door. A flashlight shone in through the slots in the door, partially illuminating the room. Kate involuntarily reached over silently and locked the door from the inside. She then backed up and waited.

The doorknob jiggled, making the most terrifying noise she had heard in months. It caused her to step backward clumsily. Her back cracked against what felt like a solid block of stone. When she had steadied herself, the doorknob shook even more violently and the door began to creak.

As the fear of discovery rose inside her, a strange sound started behind her. At first it sounded like water spraying from a nozzle, and then it sounded like hissing. Her eyes sharpened and her mind froze. She turned around, and as her eyes adjusted to the dark, she saw the form of a large, tan snake with a triangular shaped head distinct from the neck.

The cage was locked from the top, but the snake watched her closely. The cop's flashlight outlined the predator as he stalked his prey from inside his glass box. The doorknob stopped jittering as fear gripped her lungs. Not even a breath was allowed to escape as she knew the cop was listening closely. "Anyone in there? Oh, there it is."

Suddenly, the doorknob sprang back to life and the door began to open. Kate slid between the wall and tank and hid behind the large enclosure. She was out of sight for now, but she was literally inches away from her newly acquainted friend. The snake hissed at her before turning his attention to the cop.

"Oh no!" Ryan exclaimed.

From Kate's hiding place she could see the outline of Ryan's face as he grabbed his radio and pressed it to his face. "Dispatch, it's a 10-26. Just the snake. Negative on the information retrieval, heading back to 10-20."

"10-4," the radio replied.

"And what's happening with the girlfriend?" Ryan barked, his voice now receding. "She was supposed to come and collect the snake. Get onto her, will you?" His voice trailed away.

What was Ryan doing there? And what information was he trying to retrieve? Kate thought carefully, wondering if he was after evidence of the victim's crime history as well. Without warning, the hissing of the snake startled her from her thoughts, causing her to slightly jump. She hit something with her shoulder, causing the shelf above her to clatter loudly to life. Suddenly, something crashed onto the tank, shattering the lock and releasing the top of the tank. The top slowly opened, as Ryan opened the door again and trained the flashlight on the snake.

"Oh, boy," Ryan said, slowly stepping backward. With the flashlight still highlighting the snake's scaly presence, the snake slowly slithered toward Kate, still contained inside its now-topless cage. Ryan stepped forward while it crawled around the bottom of the tank, trying to close the hinged cage top. As his fingers nearly touched the lock, Kate watched when the snake quickly turned back, scaring the cop into a temporary surrender.

Kate lightly tapped on the glass. She made sure to keep it quiet to avoid Ryan's suspicion, but she knew the slimy predator heard the noise. It slowly wrapped its body in a way to allow it to strike. As it watched her intently, the snake got closer. Kate's eyes followed upward as the snake continued its ascent. Suddenly, the cover came crashing down, and Ryan secured the lock. "Snakes, why'd it have to be snakes?" he muttered as he exited the room.

Kate slouched to a sitting position behind the tank. What a relief. She waited until she was sure that Ryan had left. As she stood up, and tried to stretch her aching, cramped limbs, something long and slimy fell over her shoulders. Kate jumped to her feet, bumping her head on the shelf above, knocking an assortment of fake snakes and pet toys onto the top of the snake's tank and all over the floor.

I just experienced enough fear to last a lifetime, Kate thought in dismay.

Kate walked back out into the living room, and then saw that a yellow sticky note was stuck to her shoe. She pulled it from her shoe and read it. The scrawled writing read: *Lucy's Diner*.

"Lucy's Diner. I wonder if that place holds any clues, but I doubt it," Kate said softly. As she made her way to the window, she noticed a calendar hanging from the wall near the window. It had a large, red X circled on a particular date. Intrigued, she looked closer. It read: *Moved in*. It struck her as strange, since the circled date was only a few months back, and this man's apartment and room indicated that the victim had likely lived there for years. "Who moved in?" she asked herself.

Kate opened the window again and slipped one leg out, when the victim's phone started to ring. It sounded like a house phone, so she pulled herself back inside and walked into the living room. The phone buzzed and lights flashed, and within a few seconds, an old-fashioned answering machine beeped to life. "Please leave your message." There was silence, and then the sound of a disconnect. Then the machine kept speaking. "Saved message," it said. That was followed by a shaky voice filled with fear. "Hey man, it's me. Where have you been? Ever since you told me what you were planning, I haven't heard from you or seen you at all. You have me worried. Please, call me back. Maybe we can meet at that diner again. I just need to know you're okay."

Lucy's Diner. Maybe it would be of some value after all. Kate grabbed the sticky note. She slid down the ladder and climbed down into the street, her Amish dress flapping around her.

9

Kate approached Lucy's Diner. She clicked on the horse and took the first right into the parking lot. Surveying the area, she noticed the amount of customers must be minimal, given that there were only four cars in the large parking area.

A bell rang as she opened the door. Kate shot a practiced look around the diner. It resembled a typical breakfast restaurant. There were several booths lining the walls of the eating area, a center isle of tables and chairs, and a large kitchen, filled with staff.

Despite the lack of customers, the place looked vibrant.

Kate walked toward the hostess, a young woman with blonde hair styled in a bun, which sat atop her head like a nest in a tall tree. "How many?" she asked Kate.

"Just one, please," Kate said with a smile. The hostess motioned her to follow and sat her in the corner, at a slightly smaller booth than the rest.

"Would you like some coffee or tea to start your morning?"

"Yes, some coffee, please," Kate said.

The waitress pulled out a large menu, placed it on the table, and told Kate she would be back soon for her order. Before Kate could ask the waitress to wait, she had disappeared into the back of the diner's kitchen. The smell of eggs and bacon tickled Kate's senses as she did her best to resist the urge to place an order. She kept telling herself she was only there for information. While she flipped through the menu, Kate thought about how best to approach the questioning of the waitress.

The waitress reappeared from the kitchen and walked toward Kate with a pot of coffee in her hand. "Are you ready to place your order?"

Kate smiled and looked up from the menu. "I actually think I'm going to just have this coffee, but the food does smell delicious."

The waitress smiled back and continued filling Kate's mug with the dark, potent beverage. "Your coffee smells wonderful," she said.

"Many of our customers come just for our coffee," the waitress said.

As she turned to leave, Kate called out. "Excuse me, miss."

The waitress turned back.

"I'm actually here looking for my friend's uncle," Kate said. "He used to tell us all the time that this was his favorite breakfast place and that he was a regular. We haven't been able to get in touch with him for weeks. I was hoping maybe you or someone on staff knew him."

The waitress's face grew pale, and a sad frown overtook her previously happy demeanor. "Do you mean Ethan Jackson?"

Kate nodded.

"Oh, I'm so sorry. I'm not quite sure how to say this, but Ethan was found murdered recently."

Kate reacted to the news like a heartbroken friend hearing it for the first time. "Oh my gosh, do you know what happened? No wonder we couldn't get a hold of him."

The waitress patted her on the shoulder. "I'm so sorry you had to find out this way."

"If only we could get in touch with some of his friends and find out what happened."

The waitress nodded. "Actually, Ethan used to come here alone mostly, but in the last couple of months I've seen another man with him, many times, actually. He seemed to be a nice guy, too. I figured they must've been very good friends when they were young or something. The first time I ever saw this man meeting him here, they were hugging and acting like they hadn't spoken in years."

Kate listened carefully as the waitress spoke. "Do you by chance know his name? Or could you describe him to me?"

"He was probably in his mid or early thirties, and I never saw a ring on any of his fingers, so he's probably not married. He had brown, short-cropped hair, and he wore a pair of glasses. Let me go check the records and see if I can't find his name for you."

Kate smiled. "Thank you, so much. If we can at least find out what happened to him from his friends, it would be wonderful." She rubbed her eyes.

The waitress nodded and vanished to find the man's name.

When the waitress returned to the booth, she had a piece of notebook paper folded up in her hands. "It's against company policy to give out any personal information about our customers, but this one time I'll make an exception. I'm so sorry for your loss." She handed Kate the piece of paper.

"Thanks so much," Kate said. She finished her coffee and paid at the cashier before leaving a twenty dollar tip for the waitress.

When she reached the buggy, she pulled out the note and unfolded it. Two words were scrawled on the paper. It read: *Lucas Caden.*

The name *Lucas* resonated with her for some reason. As she tried to place his identity, it hit her out of the blue. Lucas was the last person Ethan Jackson had called before he died.

As Kate had no laptop, smartphone, or WiFi, all she could do was head to the public library to use the internet. It was only a short drive, and when Kate pulled into the parking lot, she suppressed a shudder when she looked at the building once more. The library was an old, drab building that looked as if it had been lost and forgotten. It was nearly dilapidated.

Kate thought it a marvel that the thing was still standing.

Kate walked up to the front door and walked in. As she approached the front desk, the old-fashioned hanging lights flickered off for a brief moment. When the lights were back on, Kate saw an old woman with an unkind expression on her face, sitting at the counter. Kate was disappointed to see that it was the same woman who had been here on her one and only previous visit.

The woman did not speak, but fixed Kate with a cold glare as she approached the desk. "Excuse me, I was hoping to look at some old records..."

The woman silenced her with a quick finger across her lips. "Shhhhhh."

Kate inched closer and whispered. "I need to look through some of the old phonebooks for this area."

The woman jabbed her index finger to her left. "Upstairs. Second hall," she muttered.

Kate nodded and followed the finger

upstairs. After the second isle of books, she noticed a large shelf full of old, dusty phonebooks. Kate looked through the sections until she found one of the more recent books. She flipped through the pages, using her index finger to highlight the names until she reached the Cadens. James A Caden, Thomas E. Caden, Bruce B. Caden, and several others lined the section, but no Lucas was to be seen. With a sigh, Kate set to work searching through the mountain of phonebooks.

Kate grew increasingly frustrated. She sat in the middle of the isle, which was enclosed by two long walls of books. Beside her sat at least twenty to thirty half-opened phonebooks. She dropped her face into her hands and sat in silence. How could this man not exist? Well, he did exist, she told herself, but she was just having trouble finding him. With cell phones eliminating landlines almost completely and what with so much more privacy these days, it was beginning to get more and more difficult for her to stay off the grid and still stick to this investigation. As she pulled herself to her feet, she stumbled and fell backward into the opposite wall of shelves.

"Ouch!" she yelled as her elbow slammed into the shelf, knocking some books loose, which simultaneously fell over her head, nearly collapsing her back to a sitting position.

"Quiet up there!" the voice boomed.

Kate muttered under her breath. The sting of the elbow hurt, but the knock on her head was a bigger pain. Kate started picking up the phonebooks, when she noticed one said, "Bristol County."

That must be outside city limits, because she had never even heard of that county before. Kate flipped through the pages to the C section. Her finger touched the name, *Caden*. She went down the list of names that began with C until she reached Lucas F. Caden.

That was why she had been unable find his name in any of the other phonebooks. The victim might have lived in this town, but he wasn't from here. He was from the next county, and that's where his friend Lucas must be. The record was only a few months old, so she was holding onto the hope that Lucas Caden still resided at 126 Walden Road. Kate had neither pen nor paper, so she hurried downstairs to the librarian.

The librarian's eyes slowly rolled upward. "Find what you need?" she whispered.

"Yes, I did, actually. I was wondering if you..."

Again the stern librarian lifted her finger to her lips. "Shhhhhh."

Kate whispered, "Pen and paper, please." The woman reached under her desk and slammed a small, blank sheet of paper and a pencil on the counter. "Thank you," Kate whispered before returning upstairs.

Kate jotted down the address and county, and smiled. She knew she was now one step closer to finding out what was going on and who killed Mr. Jackson, and why. Kate neatly returned each of the books to its shelf and made her way back downstairs. She strolled up to the desk and smiled politely, reaching out her hand to return the pencil. She nodded and turned to leave.

"Wait," the voice growled.

Surprised, Kate turned back to see the woman now standing in front of the desk. Both her hands were resting on her hips, and a mean look covered her face. Confused, Kate stepped closer and asked, "Yes, what is it?"

"That will be fifteen cents, please," the librarian said, in a louder tone this time.

Kate was puzzled. "Excuse me?"

"The pencil. It is fifteen cents to borrow one." The old, irritable woman pointed toward a plastic bin labeled, *Pencils: 15¢ per use*.

Kate frowned. She dug though her purse, and brought out a quarter.

"Keep the change," she said angrily. She spun on her heel and walked away, having no intention of returning to that dreadful place ever again. As she got into the buggy, she felt bad for being angry. "An Amish woman wouldn't have been angry," she said aloud, thinking of the long talk on turning the other check that one of the ministers had given at the last church meeting.

10

KATE PACED BACK and forth in her cottage, trying to think of a clever way to go and see Lucas. The words of her boss played over and over in her mind, but she just could not completely ignore the investigation. She needed to know what was going on, and why the man with the same tattoo as the hitmen she had relocated had ended up as a corpse in an Amish neighbor's pond.

Kate walked toward the Kauffman *haus*, where Beth was weeding the garden. She leaned over the fence. "Hi, Beth. Do you need anything in town? It's such a lovely day. I thought a buggy ride would do me some good and I could do your grocery shopping."

"*Wunderbaar*!" Beth exclaimed. "Well, if you are sure you wouldn't mind, I do have a list that I've been meaning to take care of. Stop by the house, and I'll have the list and money ready for you. I appreciate it. Isaac is always so busy working around the farm, so it's lovely having someone close to us who's so willing to help out here and there."

After picking up the grocery list and cash, Kate left the farm and drove to town. She tied the horse and then headed for the nearest Goodwill.

To her relief, the staff at Goodwill showed no interest in an Amish woman buying a navy blue blazer and pants, and white blouse, along with a pair of black shoes and a large tote.

Kate paid for her purchases, but now, where to change? Kate hurried to the public bathroom in the park. It was an overcast day, and the wind was increasing in ferocity, and consequently, no one was around to witness her transformation.

Soon Kate was heading toward Lucas Caden's residence in a taxi. She had no idea how this would play out—if only she had her badge and her gun. She knew the man would not speak to her willingly, and she was aware how the scenario would play out if she simply blindly approached him.

As the taxi pulled up to the nearly dilapidated Victorian home, Kate rehearsed her lines in her mind. Her plan was to offer Lucas Caden immunity from prosecution as long as he was forthcoming with information that led to an arrest in the case. She wasn't entirely certain how she would be able to keep that promise, but she stayed optimistic that the police investigating the case would not stumble onto Lucas's tracks the way she had. Kate had the taxi wait for her down the road, out of sight.

The sound of her knuckles colliding with the oak door reminded Kate of her time as a

U.S. Marshal. Life out here wasn't so bad, but she did miss being an agent. Now she was simply a former agent playing some roles. She playing a role, but she would never gain fame or praise for doing so. The sole function her acting was that of saving her own life.

The door swung open suddenly, and then disappeared from view as a middle-aged man adorned the doorway. "Yes, can I help you?"

"You most certainly can. I'm Detective Austen. I work out of the sheriff's office." She tapped her hip to give the impression that she had a firearm holstered there.

"Oh, well, come right in, Detective." Lucas led her to the living area and motioned for her to have a seat.

Kate was relieved beyond measure that the man had not asked to see her badge. "I'm here about Ethan Jackson, the homicide victim who was found recently. We have probable cause to believe you knew this person, and what you tell us might prove vital in our investigation."

What looked like fear started to sink into Lucas's appearance. His eyes retreated into beady, penetrating pupils. His smile was now all but invisible, and the tone of his skin all of a sudden looked two shades lighter. "Um, I'm not sure what you're talking about, Detective Austen."

"I was hoping we wouldn't have to do this the hard way. We know the victim was involved with organized crime. We also know that you and the victim have been seen together in recent months. I'd hate to have to get a search warrant for this place. It looks like a harsh tossing around of its contents by a squad of cops might be somewhat detrimental."

The man's shoulders sagged miserably. "It's an old home. Please. What is it you want from me?"

"Who was Ethan Jackson? What was his exact role and who did he work for?" Kate looked down at her notepad. She knew quite a bit of information already, but she needed to know everything he knew. "Why would anyone want to harm him?" she added. From the look on Lucas's face, Kate knew that she was onto something.

"Okay, I can give you a little bit of information, but that's gotta be it. I'm already too deep into this, and I can't afford to risk my life to help some cops." A terrified look covered his face. "He was a professional hitman for *The Viper*. An assassin, if you will. He carries out the hits ordered by Logan White's organization."

"Okay. And what else?"

"Well, here's where it gets kinda crazy. Ethan and I were buddies from when we were kids. I used to live in a bad part of the city and we bonded. I hadn't spoken to him in nearly twenty years, and he just suddenly appeared on my doorstep a few months back. I guess he ended up getting himself neck-deep in some trouble. He was withholding evidence for some of his contracts. He was using that evidence to blackmail the small-time crooks in hopes of getting some extra cash."

Kate's jaw dropped. "You're telling me that Ethan Jackson was taking care of marked men, and then turning around and threatening his clients with exposition?"

"Exactly. I think that's what led to him being found in the pond. He messed with the wrong people."

"You mean *The Viper*, Logan White?"

"I'm sure you've heard about a new branch of organized crime opening up nearby. He said they were *big fish*, and he kept talking about how he was going to start fishing in more dangerous waters."

The revelation was astonishing, and Kate worked hard to keep her poker face on straight. Logan White, himself, opening up a branch in town? "So, Ethan thought this new crime syndicate was going to be a bigger target? Do you know what happened after he actually tried to blackmail them?"

The man shuddered, and his face fell even

further. "Well, the last time I saw him, was about a week before he disappeared. He had come by, all panicked and freaking out. He just kept saying that he needed to get out of the country. I didn't understand why, until he told me that the new crime starting up wasn't actually new. Logan White was expanding here. His larger contractor and most vicious crime boss around right now was the one he was trying to extort. I gave him some cash to help him make an escape, but obviously it didn't help much." Lucas looked down with obvious regret.

Questions flooded Kate's mind as she thought about the actual motive. Did they kill him to silence him to take away the threat, or was it a punishment for trying to betray a kingpin? Perhaps both?

"Okay, Lucas. I do appreciate you being so open with us. I won't be pressing any charges on you, and hopefully, your information will help us solve this homicide."

Lucas nodded, his face still white.

Kate hurried back to the taxi as she thought about everything she had just learned. What would be her next step? She could hardly turn to her boss and ask his advice. At the same time, she knew that she could not keep this new information private. Something needed to be done with it, but next came the hard part. After shopping, at least. Now she had a whole different set of issues to worry about. Glancing at the list she wrestled from her pocket, more concerns clouded her already overwrought mind.

There was still a lot she had to learn about living out here, but she didn't want to get used to this life. She wanted to find the mole, solve this case, and get her life back.

11

KATE AND BETH were sitting at the old kitchen table, enjoying each other's company and a cup of hot meadow tea before finishing the dinner preparations. "I don't understand the situation with Rose and Samuel," Kate said. "It's obvious that they like each other, so why are they are pretending not to?"

"Well you see, Kate," Beth said, "it's hard to move the plow when neither horse is pulling. They just stay stuck and wait for a miracle to happen."

Kate shrugged. "I suppose you've already

given Rose hints as to how to approach Samuel?"

Beth slowly shook her head. "The thing is, she's too shy to talk to me or do something about it. I've tried to talk to her on the subject, but with zero results. Every time I say a word about it, or ask something, her cheeks blush, and she hurries away, pretending she has something important to do." Beth sighed deeply. "What can I do? I can't force her to do or say something. It's a pity that each one of them is waiting for the other to make the first step, and so they wait in vain. This dinner will have to work."

"I'm sure the dinner will work," Kate said. "It will force the two of them to stay in each other's company and actually talk to each other."

Beth simply shrugged, and Kate went to set the table, thinking how beautiful the plain setting was. When she had first arrived, she lamented her loss of television, phones, and internet, but now, she was coming to appreciate the simpler things in life. Most people in the community simply worked their land and lived from their crops and the animals they raised on their farms. They had no need for cell or conventional phones, and television was something alien to them.

The people in the community would rather speak face to face than on the phone. Kate figured that the Amish had something that *Englischers* had lost somewhere between smartphones and tablets—that soul to soul communication that bonds and creates friendships, the sort of communication she hoped to see soon around that table when Rose and Samuel were present.

"I'm nervous," Rose confided in Kate half an hour later as she paced up and down Kate's small living room. The cabin behind the main house was cramped, but the young Rose had started spending a lot of her free time with Kate, and the Kate found she really enjoyed the company. Kate really liked Rose, and they had gotten to know each other very well. Rose was young, just past eighteen, and while she had chosen to remain with the Amish community, she had expressed a few fears of doing just that with Kate. It was something she could not speak with her own parents about, as caring and understanding as they were.

And now Rose was being set up, but Kate did not think the Amish used such a term, despite the fact that they appeared very fond of matchmaking. Kate knew for a fact that Rose was attracted to Samuel, but Rose was so closed and shy about such things.

And Samuel himself was as shy as a man could be. He hardly spoke, unless it was impolite for him to stay quiet. He was tall with a square jaw, his eyes blue and shining. Kate had seen him laugh only once, but his face held such joy when he did so.

There was a knock on Kate's front door, and then it swung open and Beth stuck her head in. "Dinner is almost ready," Beth said.

Kate and Rose nodded, and then looked at one another.

"Relax," Kate said, placing her hand on Rose's shoulder. "It's just dinner."

The younger girl smiled and nodded. "Thank you for everything you've done lately."

Kate smiled. "It's my pleasure."

"You two coming?" Beth asked from the doorway, and they nodded and hurried after her. They crossed the back yard quickly and entered the Kauffman home through the back door, cutting through the kitchen. Samuel and Isaac were already seated at the table, and the men stood up as the women entered.

Kate could not help but notice Rose's reaction upon seeing Samuel. She at once smiled, an automatic gesture as if she could not restrain her joy when seeing him. Samuel greeted Kate, but when he looked at Rose, he simply nodded and forced a shy smile.

"We're going to wash up quickly," Rose told the men as she and Kate headed for the bathroom at the top of the stairs. The two women washed their hands, and then they returned to the kitchen and helped Beth set the food upon the table.

Isaac sat at the head of the table with Samuel to his right and Beth to his left. Rose sat next to her mother, and Kate sat at the other end of the table, leaving an empty seat next to Samuel. They said the usual silent prayer before mealtimes, each member of the dinner party closing their eyes and bowing their heads for a few minutes.

"*Denki*," Samuel said. "*Denki* for having me." His voice was quiet and small.

"You're more than welcome," Isaac said with a smile. "It wouldn't be kind to keep my wife's cooking all to myself."

"I haven't even kept it all to myself," Beth said, looking over at Samuel. "I've taught Rose everything I know."

Samuel smiled shyly and nodded. "I'm sure she's a *wunderbaar* cook as well," he said softly.

"Maybe she can cook next time you come over," Beth said.

Kate watched Samuel for a moment. He was shy, his head dipping down as often as it could. She looked at Rose and saw she was just as uncomfortable. It was clear that both of the young Amish folk knew exactly why they were there, and it embarrassed them.

The rest of dinner passed with ample small talk and not much left over. Kate helped Rose clear the dishes, and then she rolled up her sleeves at the sink. "I'll do the dishes," Kate said. "You can go and spend more time with Samuel."

Rose smiled softly and shook her head. "Not you, too."

"Yes, me too," Kate said with a laugh.

"I thought my parents were bad enough."

"He's a good guy. A *gut mann*. He likes you, and you like him too."

Rose nodded. "I do."

"So go and ask him if he'd like you to walk home with him."

Rose's mouth dropped open, and Kate knew she had said something wrong. As someone without much knowledge of the Amish community just trying to fit in, she did this often, but it usually could be explained away by her cover story of being in an accident and forgetting who she was.

"I couldn't ask to walk him home!" Rose exclaimed with a nervous giggle. "He would walk me home if I weren't already home."

"You're right. I meant to see if he wanted to go for a walk. Around your land maybe, before he returns home."

Rose nodded slowly. "Perhaps I will," she said. She then turned and headed back into the dining room. Ten minutes later, as Kate was washing the dishes, she glanced out of the back window and saw the two young people walking in the yard with one another. They were close together, but not touching. Kate smiled. There was something sweet to it, innocent. It wasn't like the world she had come from, and she was starting to realize that just might be a good thing.

Kate finished with the dishes and went

into the dining room, and was surprised to see Beth and Isaac still sitting at the table. Beth looked at Kate when she entered. "Have a seat, Kate, if you're in no hurry to get home."

Kate sat down across from the woman and smiled. "What are you two up to?"

"Not trouble, if that's what you're thinking," Beth with a wink, and Isaac laughed.

"So you're sitting here waiting for Rose to get back?" Kate asked.

"Maybe," Beth admitted.

"It feels like just yesterday she was four years old," Isaac said. "Running around here, getting into everything."

"And now she is out walking with the *mann* who is going to marry her," Beth said.

Kate smiled warmly at the conviction in Beth's voice. She reached over and set her hand on Beth's. "You have to let them grow up," she said.

"It's hard," Beth said.

"She'll be happier than she's ever been,"

Kate said. The two parents nodded. They sat like that for fifteen or so minutes, and then the front door opened and Rose came in.

"Samuel's heading home," she said. "He told me to thank you again for dinner."

"How was your walk?" Isaac asked.

Rose paused in the doorway and was unable to keep a wide smile from spreading across her face. "It was great," she said. "I'm going to get ready for bed."

The three at the table watched her go, and then they turned to look at one another. There was a smile on every face.

12

As daybreak approached, the animals stirred, like they did every morning. The rooster crowed, waking up every resident of the farm, both animal and human. Kate looked over at her window and smiled as the first glimpses of sun shone through. She could hear the livestock as they waited for their breakfast. This forced her to wipe away her sleepiness and roll out of bed. As she approached the wall, she stared at the dresses hanging on the pegs. With a half-hearted smile, she studied the dresses carefully. This had become her life now, but there were moments where her true self would feel like someone she was losing, like an old friend who was slipping away forever.

Kate lifted the calf-high dress in her arms and secured her bonnet with her left hand. It had been a harsh life to conform to initially, but by now she was actually enjoying her time in the preserved community. Balancing her undercover investigation into a homicide with her everyday life on the farm was difficult, but so far everything was going to plan. She finished getting ready and began preparing the feed for the animals.

As she strolled outside, she noticed Isaac was already tending the fields. He was cultivating the crops with his horse-drawn cultivator. The Amish sure were an odd bunch, but she greatly respected their values, morals, and hard work, not to mention how this couple had done so much for a complete stranger out of the kindness of their hearts.

She watched Isaac drive by and smiled, waving her hand.

Her daily chores were to maintain the animals and attend to the garden, while Isaac did the heavy duty work and Beth maintained the main house. She grabbed some feed and headed for the animal pens. Her favorite stop was always the horses, but she always saved them for last, her main reason being so she didn't have to do it twice. Isaac was using several horses to power his harvesting and cultivating equipment, so she had learned the hard way that doing the horses last was the best method. Isaac always fed them, but there was much more to caring for horses than that. She was still a city girl at heart, but being around some beautiful, majestic creatures made her feel more alive than her old job ever had.

After working the farm for hours, Kate made her way to the garden. She noticed several weeds were starting to sprout, and dropped to her knees to yank them from their intrusion. Her apron was getting dirty, and Kate idly thought that keeping her identity secret relied on blending in and playing the part.

On her knees, Kate pulled at a stubborn weed with all of her might. Her fingers began to hurt, but she refused to give up. As she struggled, she heard a familiar voice offering some help.

"You know, you could just snip that thing." Kate looked up to see Ryan standing above her. Startled, she fell back, landing softly in the cold dirt. "Oh my! I'm so sorry," he said as he rushed to her side and helped pull her to her feet.

"You scared me! You could have at least let me know you were here," she said. "And why didn't I hear your car or anything?"

"I'm so sorry. I didn't mean to scare you at all. My cruiser's parked over near the barn."

"So, may I ask what you're doing here on this fine morning? Bored and interested in learning how to work a farm?" Kate laughed.

"Oh, no, no, no," Ryan exclaimed in mock horror. "Could you ever imagine me tending crops and feeding pigs? Not my thing, sorry. I walk that thin blue line and plan to do so until my last day."

It was ironic to Kate hearing that, considering she had felt the same way not too long ago. She smiled. "So, what brings you to our farm today?" Kate crouched back down and started to dig some holes for new seed.

"I was just in the area and wanted to see how things have been around here. I'm sure homicides aren't a normal occurrence around these parts."

"That's the truth," Kate said. "I can't remember any other murders in these parts. When the news first hit, the entire community knew we were being invaded by the modern world, but I suppose you can't be who you truly are in the world without letting others do the same."

Ryan looked at her with intrigue and

smiled. "That's actually very true. You're a very smart woman."

Kate smiled and rose back to her feet. "Tell me something I don't already know," she said for a joke.

Ryan roared with laughter. "Anyway, back to business. I'm actually here to try to get some information. I've been to several of the nearby farms, including the land where the victim's body was recovered. We've gotten a few reports that a woman has been asking questions around town."

Kate's eyebrow bunched and she stood back up. "A woman?"

"Yes, you know—those people who aren't a man."

Kate's smile faded. "Ha ha, very funny," she said. "I obviously know what a woman is. I meant, what woman? What kind of questions is she asking?"

"Well, for starters, we tracked down one of the victim's old friends. He pointed us in the right direction as far as the likely suspect, but he also mentioned something that threw the investigators for a loop."

Kate couldn't help but laugh. "You really are terrible at story telling, just get to the point."

"The man told us that a woman came to see him shortly before we did. She claimed to be a police officer and asked him a barrage of questions, including several that pointed her toward the headquarters of the newly organized crime syndicate that's been invading the area."

Kate listened intently, but did not respond. She simply nodded and went back to working on the garden.

"That's not where it ends, though," Ryan continued. "We aren't certain, but it's likely that the woman who showed up at a local diner was the same person. The man we spoke to pointed us toward a diner where he and the victim often met. When we arrived there, the waitress reported that she was also questioned by a woman about the victim. The only difference here is that the woman was dressed like an Amish woman and pretended to be the victim's grieving friend instead of a cop. Something just doesn't add up. Who is this woman, and what is she up to?"

Kate rose to her feet once more and turned to the officer. "Ryan, I don't understand what you're expecting from me."

"I'm not expecting anything. I just wanted to ask you about it."

"I heard you telling me about this mystery woman, but I've yet to hear any actual questions."

Ryan sighed. "Katie, do you know the identity of the woman who's been asking questions about the murder victim?" His voice was stern, but his facial expression was warm and kind.

"Oh, well that does seem quite odd. Wouldn't you know every officer that has any involvement in your investigation?"

"That's why I'm here. We have one female officer investigating this with us, but other than Shelly, the only women who have anything to lose or gain from this case being solved are the women of this community."

Kate felt the pressure building up. "I don't know anyone outside of the Amish community aside from you and a few people in town, so I doubt I could be of any help to you in this regard. Not only do I have no idea who or why someone would be questioning townsfolk, but I'm fairly certain it's not anyone from our community. You said the woman was dressed as an Amish woman. I bet she wasn't an Amish woman at all." Kate was relieved that she could tell the truth, at least in part. She hated lying, but her very life depended on it.

"How can you be so sure?" Ryan asked.

"It goes against everything we're all about. We avoid technological advancement and the modern world, so we won't succumb to the ways of the world in the same ways that *Englischers* do. We appreciate life and nature, and while a murder would definitely hurt our community, we are not the type of people to stick our noses in the modern world just to solve a crime. Isn't that what you guys are for? Besides," she added, "we Amish do not believe in violence or retribution."

Ryan smiled. He looked at her sincerely and spoke softly. "Have you ever considered a life outside of this community?"

She stared at him. "You mean leaving the Amish way of life? Is that what you're asking?" At first, Kate was concerned that he was prying because he suspected that she could be the woman who was asking the questions, but as she watched him closely, she could see something else in his face.

"I'm sorry, Kate. I didn't mean anything by it. I was just curious to know if you ever thought about getting away from here and living a different type of life. Of course, I'm not suggesting that you would be doing yourself a disservice staying here, but we city folk could sure use someone like you in our lives."

His words warmed her, and at that moment, she felt like jumping into his arms and telling him how much she appreciated his company. He was right about the outside world being a better place for someone like her, an *Englischer*, but of course she couldn't let him know that. The Amish life was wonderful in many ways, and she had grown to appreciate it, but at the same time, she wasn't Amish and she was living a lie.

"I don't know if or when it would be possible, but I'm not opposed to the idea, in all honesty."

Ryan looked surprised. "Oh, really? That's awesome. I mean, um, I know a change of lifestyle like that would be difficult at first, but I'd be more than happy to help you out."

Kate smiled. "Do you make a habit out of going around and trying to help Amish women turn *Englischer*?" she asked.

Ryan shook his head. "No, but I'd make an exception for you." His tone was warm and gentle.

Kate's stomach turned cartwheels. Was Ryan as attracted to her as she was to him? She thought carefully before she spoke. "I've actually been thinking about leaving the Amish for some time, but I doubt it would be anytime soon. There's so much work to be done on the farm, and after all that Isaac and Beth have done for me, I could never just up and vanish. I'd have to be ready and leave on good terms."

"Very true," Ryan agreed. "The last thing you'd want to do is leave and then not be able to come back, once you realize how horrible we city folk are."

They both laughed.

"If city folk are anything like you," Kate said, "I don't see any way in the world they could be considered horrible."

13

PULLING up to the gates located at 740 Floyd Street, Kate, once again in civilian clothes, tried to peer over the large hedges, but they were there for one specific purpose, to act as a wall, preventing unsolicited eyes from gazing into the property. The gate was made of solid iron bars, and a security shack could be seen just beyond the iron barricade.

Kate had the taxi circle the neighborhood a few times to survey the scene, and eventually had him drop her about three blocks away from the mansion.

As Kate approached the wall of hedges on foot, she tried to stick her right arm through the hedges, hoping that gaining access to the property would be easier than it appeared. There was no such luck. While the hedges looked like a wall, they were actually just covering the actual barrier. A titanium wall encircled the entire premises, and hid behind the hedgerow. In an attempt to analyze the situation, Kate continued walking along the street, taking any chances she got to test the mansion's defenses for weaknesses.

Kate walked up to a bench that sat beside a small park to the west of the enclosure, looking down the street as the people of the town went about their normal business unaware of what was going on right under their noses. Logan White was close, she could feel it, and she needed to find out what was going on. Why was his organization settling in here, and what was his goal? As the thoughts occupied her mind, she noticed the gates opening up to allow a small box truck to enter.

Plastered across the truck was the logo for what looked like a catering company.

As she watched, Kate noticed two armed guards walking out from the hedge line. They circled the truck, looked underneath, and then they asked for the driver's ID. Shortly after, the larger man nodded and handed the license back, and then motioned for the truck to drive in. Perhaps if she could somehow disguise herself, she could get in the same way.

Kate's idea was great, but she realized immediately that it wouldn't work without preparation. She had to improvise, and she had to do it soon. Walking toward the gate, she wasn't sure what to do, but the thoughts were racing through her mind. As she got closer, the gate slowly started to open. The same truck was now pulling out, but the men were once again inspecting it. Coming to a stop halfway into the road, the truck was still partially obstructing the gate, ensuring it would stay open until the men were finished with their routine check.

As the man on her side of the truck bent over to look underneath, Kate quickly but silently jumped through the gate and then slid into the first bunch of bushes she came across. It was already starting to get dark. What could she do now? Kate watched silently from her hiding place as she struggled to think of an idea.

Kate had counted seventeen guards patrolling the exterior of the mansion, which was set far back on the land. They all had firearms and looked dangerous, but she knew this would be her only chance to get some information on Logan White and his organization. Fear started to creep in, but her training as a Federal Agent halted it.

As time ticked away, one of the guards patrolled close to her location. He walked slowly, kept alert, and never kept his focus on one area for more than a few seconds. Kate studied him carefully. The man walked away, but moments later patrolled back toward her. This was her chance. Kate scooped up a handful of rocks from under the bush and tossed them a few yards in front of him.

As soon as the pebbles crashed into the grass, the man reacted to the sound. Looking back and forth furiously, he kneeled down to examine where he thought the object had landed. Kate watched as he picked up some dirt in his right hand before dumping it back onto the earth. Almost immediately, his radio was making noise.

"Yo, it's Liam. Have you guys heard anything or seen any movement on the surveillance system? I think we might have an intruder."

After a brief silence and what sounded like someone grabbing the radio on the other end, a man spoke sternly. "Liam, what happened?" The raspy, authoritative voice boomed over the handheld radio.

"Sir, something just doesn't feel right. I heard some kind of noise and when I turned toward it, it looked like a rock or something was hitting the ground. It was like someone was trying to distract me." Turning around, the man stared right into the bush where Kate was hiding. "Oh snap, I think I found the culprit."

"Liam, you get that intruder to me, right now." The fury heard over the speaker terrified Kate. Her heart pounded as the goon reached into the bush. His hand touched her skin and gripped tightly around her right shoulder. She stood up and surrendered reluctantly, but only because she knew it was her only option.

"Boss, I got her," he reported through his radio.

"Her? Bring that woman to my office. Do not let her get away, or you'll be sorry you did." The line went silent and the large, muscular man next to Kate took a deep gulp in fear.

"Yes, sir!" His words were left unanswered.

As they hurried through the yard toward the distant mansion, the thug kept pushing Kate forward with the butt of his weapon.

Kate nearly lost her balance a few times, and took care to keep from stumbling to the ground. The last thing she wanted to do right now was to be completely defenseless, even though she knew she already was.

"Let's go. Keep yourself together." His words stung, but she kept on.

As they approached the entrance to the house, two guards in black suits held even larger weapons than the others. "Business?"

"The boss wants this intruder."

The man on the right side of the door stepped forward. "All right. Go back on watch and I'll bring her to White." Her former captor nodded and backed away, leaving her in the presence of another man.

When Kate entered the mansion, she was amazed by what she saw. Beautiful paintings and portraits lined the long halls of the first floor of the building.

"Keep your mouth closed and your eyes forward," the guard said. "The boss doesn't like to be disrespected, so I suggest you let him do most of the talking."

Her mind drifted back to her days as an agent, but she could hear the voice of her boss echoing in her ears. "Play the part." She knew White wouldn't have a clue who she was, but even a hint of her training and he'd sniff her out like a bloodhound chasing after the scent of a wild boar. The plan was laid out before her eyes: play the role of the farm girl and let him think she accidentally stumbled onto his land.

As they continued to delve deeper into the vast mansion, the guard nudged her toward a flight of steps. As they ascended the stairs, they came upon a water fountain in the center of the hallway. Kate could not help but notice the beauty of such a violent, dangerous place. It reminded her of a volcano that was due to erupt at any moment.

The two kept on until Kate was facing a large set of white doors. Four men outlined the section of the hallway. She was able to analyze the situation and noticed that unlike the other men she had seen so far, these four were wearing bulletproof vests under their suits. This was Logan White's office. It had to be.

The four guards stepped aside, and one of them spoke into his radio. "Boss, they're here." The response was difficult to understand due to the large volume of static, but the man must have understood the order. "Yes, sir." With those words, the doors opened, and she was ushered into the office.

In the large room sat three desks. One to her left, one to her right, and the biggest one lined the wall parallel to the doorway. On the smaller desks sat two men counting stacks of money. Kate kept her eyes straight and held back any words that threatened to escape her mouth. Behind the central desk was a man in his mid-fifties or so. He had what appeared to be a scar over his left eye and he wore a very nice suit. He poked out his cigar in an ashtray and pulled his chair closer to the desk.

"Hello there. Do you mind if I ask what a pretty little thing like you is doing snooping around my property?" The tone of his voice was unnerving.

"I, um, I don't even know where I am. I was walking my dog and he just ran away from me. I had the leash in my hand, but he yanked it right out. I think a truck was pulling out or something and he got through your gate when it was open. I saw his leash disappear around the hedges and chased after him. I didn't even notice the guards at first, but as soon as I did, I hid in a bush. I was terrified." Kate kept a straight face and even showed sincere emotion as she spoke.

White turned to the guard. "Have you or your men seen any dogs running around the premises?" The man shook his head. "Very well. Have them start a search. As for you, my lady, who are you?"

When Kate started to speak, White interrupted, looking at her guard once again.

"Did she have any ID or anything on her when she was found?"

"No, sir. She had nothing on her at all. Not even a cell phone."

"Interesting." He turned back to Kate. Do you make a habit out of going for long walks without a phone or a wallet?"

Keeping the fear at bay, Kate responded in an earnest tone. "I'm sorry sir, but I'm still new to city life. I was just visiting a friend a few blocks away and Ruffles had to go out."

The boss' beady eyes felt like lasers on her skin. "Ruffles?"

"My dog, sorry."

"Very well. If you're not a city girl, what would you call yourself?"

"A farmhand. I live on a farm and tend the crops, feed the animals. I've grown up doing that all my life."

"So a little farm girl found her way into the heavily guarded lion's den? Sounds like a bad joke." Logan leaned forward, cupping his chin in one hand. "We don't take kindly to trespassers. Let us find your little dog and then we'll have another chat."

His cold demeanor chilled Kate to her core. Kate bowed her head and kept her focus toward the ground.

"Take her to the hold. Make sure she gets some food and water. I might be ruthless, but I'm not a monster."

White's words trailed off as the doors closed behind her and the goon. "You did good in there, kid. Just keep your nose down and do what you're told like in there, and he'll let you go. We just have to be sure you're not a threat."

"A threat? To whom? What could I do that would harm you guys?"

"Listen, I don't know what you've seen or what you haven't, but you're in over your head. Tread lightly, or you might not make it out of this."

They made their way back downstairs to an old wooden door that had a large metallic lock and chain on the outside.

"You're home," the man said with half a smile cracked across his face. It took the man at least two minutes to unlock the heavily secured door. He nudged her inside.

In the square room sat a single chair that looked to be cemented into the floor. Two long chains with cuffs lay on the sides of the chair.

14

DARKNESS. That's all there was.

After the guard had shut the door, Kate was left shackled in a small room with no windows. She knew it would be no use screaming. Nobody would hear her, at least nobody who would be willing to help. The only solace she found was in the form of the light shining underneath the heavily barricaded door. Fear clouded her mind as panic swallowed her whole.

"What a nightmare!" she said aloud. A large part of her was hoping that somehow

Ryan would show up to save her, but then her cover would be blown and everything would just get even worse.

Kate figured there had to be a way out of there. She ran her eyes across the room, surveying every inch that the small fragment of light allowed her to see. There was nothing around her but an empty room.

The one thing that her career had taught her was never to let the fear take over. Just a stupid joke and a small laugh could be the difference between giving up and overcoming the odds. Suddenly, she thought back to one phrase that White had said. *"Make sure she gets some food and water. I might be ruthless, but I'm not a monster."*

Kate was sure this man was a monster, but that wasn't the part of his statement on which she focused at that very moment. *Water and food*—she would have a chance to escape if she could overcome the guard who would be delivering her meal. The only problem standing in her way, however, was the fact that tightly bound shackles secured both her ankles.

Kate wondered what the Amish would do in this situation. Kate was pondering her problem, when the lock on the door turned.

This was it. She had to be ready. As the sound of metal scraping against the door grated on her nerves, she dropped her arms to the sides of her body and rolled her fingers into the tightest fists possible. Then, she slid backward in the chair and pretended to be lifeless. Her head fell to her chest, and silence engulfed the small dungeon.

The sound of the large, iron door opening echoed throughout the chamber, and light shone on Kate, but she did not so much as flinch. She heard the guard's voice. "Hey, you. Wake up!" Kate heard him as he approached her seemingly lifeless body. "Hey, lady! What are you doing?"

Silence answered his questions. She could feel his breath on her face as he examined her. He gently grabbed her shoulder and carefully shook her body. "The boss is insistent you eat and drink. Please, wake up, lady!"

Without any warning, Kate lunged to her right, throwing the man off guard and causing him to fall forward onto her. She raised her left hand under his chin and cradled the back of his head with her right hand. Then, she pushed with every ounce of strength she could muster into that left hand, pinching his nerve and rendering him unconscious. "Always protect your pressure points, man!" Kate uttered quietly under her breath.

Leaning forward, she searched the body for the key to her chains. The man's weight was painful, and he was difficult to reposition, but she eventually uncovered the key in one of his pockets. Once Kate had gently pushed the unconscious guard off her, she wasted no time in unlocking the cuffs around her ankles and searching the body once more. She found a stun-gun but no pistol. Kate grabbed the stun-gun, tucked it into her waistband, and exited her prison.

Kate peered cautiously around the corner, but she saw nothing but a long, empty hallway. She needed to find the exit, and she wasn't even sure where to start. As Kate left the safety of the room in which she had been locked, she heard what sounded like two men having a conversation. She crouched close to the floor and put her ear to the corner of the wall.

"Hey man, where's Perry? He was just supposed to give that girl we caught some food and then take over my post. I need to get outta here to get home before my wife does."

"I don't have a clue, bro. I'll keep an eye out here until you return if you wanna go see what's up."

Kate heard footsteps drawing near. Slowly falling back, she used her hand to guide her as she continued along the wall. Kate found what felt like an opening, and then she disappeared into a broom closet. The footsteps grew even louder.

Like a tiger hiding in the darkness, she

watched the guard as he slowly passed by, clueless that he was about to become prey to his own victim. As his back faced her, Kate lunged up from the closet and jabbed him in his side with the taser, dropping him to his knees immediately. The loud thud drew the attention of the other goon.

Retreating once more into her cubby hole, she took out the next guy using the same technique, while he checked his unconscious friend. Kate slowly dragged both men into her former prison and locked all three guards in their own holding cell.

As Kate made her way through the maze of mansion walls and rooms, she finally saw her chance at freedom. The door was most likely guarded on the outside, and this worried her. As she slowly stepped toward the exit, a set of footsteps crashed down behind her.

Kate saw a guard on patrol making his way down the steps directly behind her. Without thinking, she jumped beside the staircase and waited. The man carried a large, automatic

rifle nestled in between both of his arms.
After reaching the first floor, the man slowly
walked toward the door, glancing out the
windows that lined it. Silently, Kate crept
backward up the stairs, maintaining a
constant eye on the guard. When he was out
of sight, she turned around on the second
floor landing.

Suddenly, a pair of hands gripped her, and
the arms of her new captor grabbed her
shoulders. "Where do you think you're going?
White is gonna be very unhappy. How'd you
get up here anyway? Weren't you locked in the
hold?"

Kate refused to give the guard any
satisfaction, and kept silent.

The doors to the central office burst open
as the guard pushed Kate forward. The
disturbance caused everyone in the room to
stop what they were doing and stare at the
two visitors. The only noise that she could
hear came from Mr. White. His fiery eyes
looked up at her, as anger boiled over his

visage. "You know better than to walk into my office uninvited," he snapped at the guard.

"I'm sorry, sir. I caught this wench trying to escape and thought you'd want to see her immediately."

"You could have called it in over the radio." The anger seemed to dissipate slowly as he spoke to his guard. "Well, I suppose you just did me a huge favor, so this time you'll walk out of here. Next time, however, make sure you call it in first." His stern voice appeared to strike fear into the guard. The guard nodded to his boss and left the room, leaving Kate to face the man by herself. Logan whipped his hand around in the air at the others in the room, as if to tell them to leave. Everyone except Kate and White silently left the room. The large doors closely tightly behind her.

"So, how did you get in here?"

"I told you. I chased my dog."

"No. How did you get in my office right now?"

Kate put a confused expression on her face, to imply that she was brought to his office against her will. "I was dragged here."

"No. Listen to me when I ask you a question. You're really starting to get on my nerves. How did you get out of the holding cell and make it past all of the guards on the first floor?"

Kate thought quickly. "The guard who brought me my food said he felt bad for me, so he unlocked my chains and helped me get to the front door, before he took off in a different direction. Once I realized there were guards standing right outside of it though, I unintentionally ran backward into the man who brought me to you."

"Very well. Looks like I have another weed to yank out of my garden." White stood up and slowly walked over to her. "So, a farm girl wanders onto my property, interrupts my business, and then tries to escape? What do you think an appropriate punishment would be for that?"

The man looked at Kate and folded his arms, as if undecided what to do.

In a flash, Kate lunged at White. She pulled the stun-gun from her pocket with and thrust it at him. The two fell backward together, and she ended up on top of him, keeping the pressure against his skin. After a brief struggle, Logan's body fell limp, and Kate climbed back to her feet.

Now what?

At that moment, Kate heard a commotion coming from outside. She rushed to the window, and saw several cop cars lined up inside of the mansion's gate. Kate looked around for a way of escape, and saw that one of the windows had a fire escape strapped to it. She lifted the window and then slowly shut it, just as the doors to the office opened.

Safely hidden from view just outside the window, Kate glanced down to see how high up she was. The ladder would get her to freedom, but just as she was about to make her way down, she heard a familiar voice from the room.

"What on earth happened in here?"

Kate peeked around the window and watched as Ryan crouched near the body of White, feeling for a pulse. "He's alive," Ryan said to another officer. "Looks like we might have ourselves a vigilante. He must be a tough one too, if he took out this guy."

His radio buzzed. "Sir, we have three guards unconscious in what looks like some sort of dungeon or something."

"All right, I'll be right down. Let me cuff this guy and make sure he finds his way to a cruiser."

Kate smiled. She turned to the ladder and slid down to safety. The grounds were covered with police, but she was able to sneak toward the gates unnoticed. Kate slipped into the darkness of night.

15

Battered and likely to bruise, Kate limped a little as she walked away from the hectic scene at Logan White's mansion. Sirens and chaos could still be heard in the distance as she approached her hiding place. She pulled out the burner cell phone she had bought recently for the purposing of calling taxis, and called one now.

Kate let out a sigh of relief. It was all over now. Logan would be arrested, and Kate was confident the police had followed the cell phone trail all the way both to Lucas Caden's residence and then the mansion. All she had to do was get a taxi into town, change back into Amish clothes, and call another taxi, to hide her trail.

When the taxi drove past the vicinity of the mansion, Kate glanced to her left to see numerous cop cars and news vans littering the street. Someone was being escorted out in handcuffs as the taxi waited at the lights. It was Logan White. He looked to be resisting and arguing with Ryan, who appeared to be struggling to hold the suspect in his custody. The light turned green, but she continued watching as another police officer assisted Ryan in throwing the kingpin into the back of a cruiser.

All went smoothly, and Kate finally arrived at her cabin under the cover of night, with the Kauffman household none the wiser to her actions.

The next morning, Kate was working in the garden. Rose was on a buggy ride with Samuel. The very thought made Kate smile widely, even though her face ached. In fact, every part of her body ached.

Kate watched with some trepidation as a police cruiser drove toward the house. Ryan climbed out of the car, a smile decorating his handsome face. "Good morning," he said.

"Good morning," Kate responded, wondering what Ryan was going to say.

Ryan's smiled widened. "Are Isaac and Beth here? I wanted to speak to you all at the same time."

"No, they're gone to town," Kate said. "What news do you have?"

"We solved the murder of Ethan Jackson last night."

Kate leaned forward and did her best to look surprised. "Really? Who did it?"

"The victim was a hitman for the suspect, Logan White. We received the victim's cell phone in the mail from an anonymous source, and used that to track down a friend of his."

"Wow, that's wonderful," Kate said. "What

a lucky break with the phone. Come to the porch, and I'll make us some meadow tea."

Ryan followed Kate to the porch, and he sat on one of the comfortable chairs. Kate soon returned with some meadow tea and plate of whoopie pies, which she set in front of Ryan, before taking her seat next to him.

Ryan ate a whoopie pie before speaking. "That was good." He turned to smile at Kate. "The friend led us to this guy, White, who has known affiliations in organized crime. We have reason to believe he was opening up a branch nearby. The evidence shows that the vic was embezzling or extorting money from the boss, so he had his goons take him out for his crimes. A hitman and crime boss are both off the streets, not to mention all of his goons are going to be joining him in prison. Plus, the station and the state will each get a split of the resources he just left behind."

"That's great, it really is. I feel so much safer already." Kate smiled, sincerely relieved to hear the news. "That was good of the victim's friend to help the police. Is he in trouble?"

"No," Ryan said, "but why the interest?"

Kate was relieved that Lucas Caden would not be charged. After all, she had implied to him that he wouldn't be. Yet her question had aroused Ryan's suspicions. Kate thought fast. "It's nice when people help the police," she said, silently chastising herself for not thinking of something more convincing to say.

Nevertheless, Ryan appeared to be distracted. His expression suddenly changed and he seemed to be clouded in deep thought. "Hmm," he said. "I didn't even put it together before."

"What?" Kate asked in surprise.

"The phone. I had chalked it up to just some random person finding the phone and sending it to the police in lieu of a lost and found or something."

"That was probably the person's intention," she added.

Ryan shook his head. "No, it definitely

wasn't. It was the same person who knocked out Logan White moments before we even arrived. He even used the fire station as the returning address to throw us off. You should have seen those firefighters when I showed up, and asked them who found the murder victim's cell phone."

Kate's brow furrowed as her concern increased.

"What person? What are you talking about? The crime boss was already unconscious when you arrived?"

Ryan nodded. "And that's not all. This man infiltrated a walled mansion, complete with at least twenty armed guards, cameras, and a security booth at the gate, and then he still managed not to be identified. Even Logan White wouldn't say who did this."

The revelation surprised her. "Maybe he doesn't know who it was. The guy probably knocked him upside the head pretty hard or something."

Ryan shook his head. "No, I'm sure he

remembers everything. I could tell when I questioned him. I kept asking him how one man could sneak into his mansion, take out some of his guards, and then escape without being so much as seen. He laughed hard, like I'd said something overly funny. Then, he said something even weirder." Ryan paused and repositioned himself on the rocker.

"What was that?" Kate asked.

"He said, 'One man could never have done this.' So, the logical follow up was to ask how many people were involved. He kept saying only one was involved. It made so sense at all."

"Maybe he did get a harder knock on the head than you thought," Kate said.

Ryan shrugged. "Perhaps."

"I don't see why you're taking it so hard though," Kate said. "Did the man steal some of the evidence or money or something?"

"No, I'd say he's a vigilante, and he's a man in trouble."

Kate was confused. "Why would he be in trouble? With the police, you mean?"

Ryan shook his head. "No. Logan White doesn't suddenly have amnesia or something. He's withholding the vigilante's identity for one reason; so he can be the one that finds him first."

"I'm sure Mr. White will be in prison long enough to forget about it," Kate said, "and when he does get out, I'm sure all you police officers will be keeping an eye on him to make sure he doesn't come back here anyway."

"Of course, but without knowing the identity of this vigilante, we don't know who his target will be. The only clue to the person's identity is a stun gun that was left behind at the mansion."

Kate's heart sank into her stomach. The stun gun: she had forgotten it. Kate had not worn gloves to the mansion, and she was afraid that she had left fingerprints behind. She was in the habit of wiping off fingerprints, but everything had happened so fast, that she could not even remember if she had wiped them off after Logan White had gone down.

Kate took a deep breath and closed her eyes. She had to compose herself and act normal.

Ryan was still talking. "I just got off the phone with the crime lab. They found a partial print on the Taser gun. The tech's examining it now. He said he had two patterns matched in AFIS, but the rest has been difficult due to the quality of the print left behind."

"What does that mean?" Kate asked, although she already knew the answer.

"It means it's inconclusive right now, and unless he can make several more matches, the print is as good as useless."

Kate rose to her feet, prompting Ryan to follow. "I need to get on with the farm chores. If you'd like to keep me company, you're more than welcome to."

Ryan nodded in agreement and followed her down the steps. Kate scooped up a basket from the table before they left.

Kate walked over to the chickens, and

checked their water supply. She looked at the animals and smiled. "Hey guys, are you ready for some treats?" She dumped a handful of corn into their yard and watched as they dug through the hay for the delicious bonus to their meal.

Ryan watched her with a smile. "You really love those things, don't you?"

"The chickens?"

"No. I meant the animals in general. I can tell you've grown up around livestock most of your life."

Kate was unable to suppress a giggle. If only he knew the truth.

"It's somewhat of an endearing quality," Ryan said.

"Somewhat?" Kate echoed.

Ryan laughed, and at that moment, their eyes met. A warmth engulfed her as she studied his eyes. Suddenly, his phone rang, interrupting the tender moment.

"Hello? Yes, this is the detective on the vigilante investigation. Hey, Steve."

Kate listened intently to Ryan's side of the phone call.

"So, did you end up getting a hit on that print?" Several moments passed before he spoke again. "Are you sure? That doesn't make any sense." Ryan's expression dimmed, and he looked back at Kate. His eyes seemed to pierce into her. He turned away and continued his conversation. "Make sure you save that print. If anything happens to it, I am holding you directly responsible." After a few more seconds, the phone call ended, and Ryan turned around.

"So?" Kate asked. "What did he say?"

Ryan slowly looked at her and spoke softly. "There weren't enough matches for the fingerprint to be admissible, so I just asked him to secure the print in case it can be used as a secondary identifier in case we hear from this vigilante again. Let's just hope this man is really on our side if he decides to stick his head out into the world again."

Kate smiled. "You know, you should be

thanking the man, instead of being so concerned. He did help you take down one of the biggest crime bosses around, didn't he?"

Ryan smiled. "I guess he did. Looks like I have a guardian angel watching over me. First the tips that led us there, and then the guy was gift wrapped, waiting for me." Ryan laughed. "You know, I never believed in angels until you moved to this farm."

16

KATE LEFT her small cottage in the early
morning. There were droplets of dew on the
grass, reflecting the orange light of dawn. Her
breath slid visibly out of her, hanging in a
white cloud in front of her lips before fading
away into nothingness. She was dressed in an
Amish dress, and had a shawl wrapped around
her shoulders. So it was done, the crime
syndicate had been dismantled in town, and
everything should be going back to normal.

But still, Kate felt on tenterhooks. She had

woken earlier than usual, her heart racing. She needed closure of some sort, and she thought she knew just where she needed to go for that. And so she started walking, moving to the road and making her way to her destination, just as others were beginning to rise from their beds.

She went toward the Kauffman pond where she often went to think and contemplate, and in recent times, to pray. Kate climbed carefully over the fence that separated the field from the road, and then stepped lightly through the long grass, and across the soft dirt.

At the pond, Kate paused, looking at the beauty of the water and the long green grass that grew along its edge, and the brown reeds that were growing at random within them.

A bullfrog croaked, a long low sound in the morning, like a sad song. A few dragonflies were up early, darting here and there over the surface of the water. A chill breeze blew, sending the tips of the reeds and grass bobbing back and forth, and slow ripples moving across the top of the water, forcing the six or so lily pads that called the pond home along one side of the pond, near the muddy bank.

Kate folded her arms over her chest and clutched her shoulders, trying to stay warm, but failing. Still, this was where she needed to be, and she closed her eyes and listened to the sounds of the pond while she reflected on what had happened the last month or so.

Kate thought about the bad guys of course, and she knew that was a simplistic way to think of them, merely as bad guys, but she couldn't help it. That's what they were. She had always thought of them like that, even back in WITSEC.

Back in WITSEC. It was strange to think like that. It made it sound as though she wasn't ever going to go back. It sounded like WITSEC was her past. But she knew that wasn't true. She would be able to leave the Amish community some day.

And thinking of leaving brought a new pang of pain to her heart. She had really come to love the people she had gotten to know in the community. They had all made her feel like family, had gone out of their way to do so. And the idea of leaving really did make her sad.

Kate just happened to turn and look back to the road, and she was surprised to see a police cruiser parked there near the fence, and then in the field halfway between the pond and the road, and coming closer with every step, was Ryan.

She wondered what the cop was doing out here. She turned fully and waited for him to reach her, unable to hide a smile as he finally did.

"Kate," he said, nodding a bit.

"Officer."

"Call me Ryan, you know that."

"Not many people get to be called Officer. Don't you prefer it?" she asked in teasing tone.

Ryan laughed and shook his head. "Not really. Not from my friends."

"I'm glad to know you think we're friends," Kate said.

"Aren't we?" Ryan asked.

"Of course we are," Kate said. She decided to change the subject. They were getting a little too close to flirting for her taste, and there was nothing she could do about it as long as she was posing as an Amish woman. "You're far from home, aren't you?"

Ryan laughed and shrugged. "I was coming to see Isaac, and you, and a few others," he said. "I didn't know you would be out here, though. I almost drove right by you."

Kate nodded. "I come down to the pond to think and pray," she said.

Ryan smiled. "I like to have time to myself to think and pray," he said, "after I wrap up a case. It's therapeutic."

Kate nodded. "It is. So what did you want to tell us?"

"I told you everything yesterday, but I wanted to see if Isaac and Beth had any questions."

"Isaac and Beth will like that."

"Can I ask you something?" Ryan asked, his face turning stern, and Kate knew they were about to get back into the territory she was trying to avoid, but maybe with them, there just wasn't the option to avoid it.

"Yes," Kate said, her stomach clenched.

"Have you thought any more about leaving the community? The Amish community?"

Kate looked at the young man. He looked back at her, and there was no question there was a strong attraction between them, one they both felt, and one on which they both wanted to act. And yet they couldn't date, not while Kate was Amish, even if she wasn't really Amish.

Kate smiled and nodded her head. "I have," she said.

"And?"

"I will leave."

Ryan's face crinkled into a thousand smiles. "When?"

Kate smiled again and reached out, placing her hand on the cop's arm. "I don't know. When I can. When I'm ready."

Ryan nodded. "Well, when you do, would you like to go to dinner with me?"

Kate knew she was smiling too much, but another smile came, and she didn't stop it. She nodded. "Yes," she said.

"Great." Ryan turned to face the pond, and Kate turned as well. They stood like that for a long while, watching the morning sun continue to rise over the horizon, brightening the day as it did so. It brought more warmth too, and as it warmed up, their breath wasn't visible anymore, and Kate didn't need the shawl. She pulled it from her shoulders and folded it over her arm.

The bullfrog made an appearance, hopping out from under a clump of the long grass and sunning himself on the muddy bank. He croaked loudly, and when Ryan took a step toward him, he leaped away, flinging himself into the pond water. The couple on the shore watched the ripples fade away.

Kate turned. "I should go back," she said.

"I can give you a ride," Ryan said.

Kate laughed and shook her head. "Thanks, Ryan, but I need to walk and think and pray some more."

"Well, I guess I'll see you around, Kate," Ryan said.

"You will," she replied.

Kate turned and walked away from the man, and away from the pond. She headed for the woods, intending to take the shortcut back home. She forced herself not to look back at Ryan, to see if he was watching her, even though she wanted to. Instead, she kept moving forward, into the woods, although the man was on her mind.

A trip to the pond was just what she had needed. She could let the case go now, everything that had happened, the dead man with the viper tattoo, and *The Viper* himself. Now new thoughts flooded into her mind, and they all had to do with Ryan.

But if Kate were to be honest with herself, thinking about Ryan wasn't too bad, after all.

The Next (and Last) Book in this 3 Book Series
Safe Hearts

U.S. Marshal, Kate Briggs, is still posing as an Amish woman. When the cousin of one of the Amish Knitting Circle ladies is accused of murder, Kate once again throws herself into the investigation. However, the criminal looking for her has finally tracked her down to the small Amish community in which she is hiding. How will Kate protect not only herself, but the entire community, from the desperate criminal?

When Kate's identity is revealed, how will everyone react, especially Detective Ryan Weaver?

ABOUT RUTH HARTZLER

Ruth Hartzler spends her days writing, gardening, walking her dog, and thinking of ways to murder someone. That's because Ruth is a best-selling author of cozy mysteries. She is best known for her #1 best-selling 2015 series, Safe House, featuring a WITSEC agent hiding in the Amish community, and for apologizing to strangers when her dog slobbers all over them at the park.

The recipient of several All Star Awards (author and book), Ruth is thrilled to connect with her readers, all of whom love the same clean and wholesome stories she does.

www.ruthhartzler.com

Made in the USA
Middletown, DE
19 June 2020

33R00113